Forever 🌹 *Romances*

LOVE'S FULL CIRCLE

Lurlene McDaniel

is an imprint of
Guideposts Associates, Inc.
Carmel, NY 10512

"Therefore everyone who hears these words of mine, and acts upon them, may be compared to a wise man, who built his house upon the rock.

And the rain descended, and the floods came, and the winds blew, and burst against the house; and yet it did not fall, for it had been founded upon the rock" (Matthew 7:24–25).

CHAPTER 1

"IT'S GOING TO BE A BRIGHT and beautiful scorcher, today in the Washington, D.C. area, folks. But we'll be doing our part to keep you cool and mellow here at FM 104." The cheerful voice of the radio announcer caused Julie Kreel to look up at her kitchen clock. "6:45 . . ." she muttered. She was running late. If she didn't get into the flow of the Beltway traffic by 8:15, she'd never make it to her office by nine o'clock.

But she lingered over her morning coffee, pensive, unable to motivate herself into meaningful movement. Julie ran her hand over the smooth pages of her open Bible. "At least I've had *some* quiet time with You, Lord," she said aloud. It was a well-established habit . . . this early morning ritual of rising, brewing coffee, reading her Bible, and spending a few moments in devotion before her hectic, workaday schedule began. And the habit of starting the day with God had proven effective and rewarding to her over the years.

A soft purring and the brush of fur against her legs caused her to look beneath her antique pine breakfast table. "Hi, Hector," Julie crooned at her big white Angora cat. "Am I ingoring you, old fellow?" She

7

stroked the cat's sleek head. "Why can't I get moving today? What's wrong with me?" she asked her feline companion. Hector meowed.

Sunlight collected in bright, buttery pools on the breakfast table, and Julie glanced out the kitchen window of her apartment at the green leafed trees, already limp and listless in the gathering morning heat. Maybe she needed a few more minutes of prayer. . . .

The music on the radio ended and the announcer's rich, melodious voice broke through Julie's lethargy. "It's 6:55 a.m., September 12th, and here are the day's headlines." *September 12th!* Julie's heart lurched and her eyes flew to the calendar hanging against a brightly papered kitchen wall. The date all but leaped off the page at her . . . bold, black, accusatory.

The top of the calendar displayed a picture of colorful meadow flowers, dainty, caught rippling and bowing by a camera's eye. Below the photograph, script letters proclaimed: "This is the Day the Lord has made!" But all Julie saw now was the date. September 12th. That date, heavy with personal meaning, burdened with bitterness and heartache.

September 12th. It would have been her sixth wedding anniversary. Instead, it marked the fifth summer of her divorce.

With sudden vehemence, Julie scraped her chair across the tiled floor. Hector hissed, arched his back, and scampered through the doorway. Julie tossed what was left of her coffee into the sink, shut her Bible, and hurried to her bedroom, pushing the sad and bitter memories out of her mind.

"Stop it!" she warned herself as she quickly made her bed and then rummaged through her closet for something to wear. "You're being a fool!" she admonished. "It's just a date on the calendar. Good grief, Julie, September 12th comes every year."

In her lime green bathroom, Julie artfully applied her make-up with quick, practiced strokes. But gentle, nudging cramping in her abdominal area caused her to pause and mentally calculate the reason for the persistent muscle spasms. "Just what I need!" She groaned with renewed irritation at her pretty black-haired, brown-eyed reflection in the bathroom mirror.

It was one more reminder of the direction her life had taken over the past few years. One more reminder of what should be, instead of what *was*. She could have been a mother by now. If only. . . .

Twelve-year-old Julie sat wide-eyed on her bed, staring at her mother's smiling face. It had happened to her! During the night. The gentle passage from childhood to womanhood. She swallowed, awed and scared at the immensity of having become a woman while she had slept.

"Julie, God has given you a wonderful gift," Ruth Kreel said softly, clasping her daughter's slim fingers. "It's the most precious thing you have. It's yours and yours alone. Don't give it away lightly."

Julie nodded, slightly mystified by her mother's fervent words. Ruth continued, staring deep into her daughter's expectant brown eyes, turned up nose, and full, curved lips. "You're a Christian girl, Julie. You know right from wrong. You've gone to church and Christian school all your life. You know what the Lord expects of you."

Julie agreed, solemnly, the impact of her budding womanhood pushing aside the barefoot days of summer in her mind. "God created man and woman for His pleasure, Julie. But he surely meant for man and woman to find pleasure in one another, too." Her mother's words caused Julie to blush crimson.

Once, in the fifth grade, Billy Nelson had held her down and kissed her. It hadn't been exciting. In fact, it had only made her mad! "You're a very pretty girl, dear," Ruth said, stroking Julie's cheek lovingly. "You will be tempted, sorely tempted," she emphasized causing Julie's denial of "Not me!" to die on her tongue.

"Don't ever think that Satan's going to come at you

*looking ugly and untempting," Ruth continued, her voice
serious, but warning. "No . . . sometimes, Julie, the
Devil has blue eyes."*

*Julie nodded, yet it was years before she fully under-
stood exactly what her mother had meant. And then it
was too late. . . .*

Julie finished dressing, scanned the interior of the
spacious apartment one last time, patted Hector absently, snatched up her slim leather briefcase, and ran
for the door. It was 8:25. She was going to be late. Her
mood darkened even more.

Traffic was murder. Julie eased her red sports car
into the slow-moving stream of morning commuters.
The rich smell of the leather seats mollified her a little.
She realized that the car was a wanton luxury. She
loved it. "Besides," she muttered under her breath,
"what else have I got to spend my money on."

As head copywriter for Denton and Bowles Ad
Agency, Julie Kreel made good money. After her church
tithe and her living expenses, she had plenty left over
for the car payments. Yet, this morning, she had wished
she had the foresight to leave the top on the car, then
she could have turned on the air conditioning and not
arrived at the office sticky and soggy. "Isn't anything
going right today?"

A young executive in the car next to her smiled appreciatively and tipped his head at her. She flushed and
ignored his blatant flirtations. *Probably has a wife and
two kids at home,* she thought bitterly. "Men! I'll bet
there's not a faithful one in the earth's lot of them!"

Julie managed to find a parking space in a lot three
blocks from her office. She walked the distance swiftly,
her navy heels clicking over the pavement, her pale
blue linen skirt swishing against her slim thighs and
hips.

"Morning, Donna," Julie called to the red-haired
receptionist as she entered the plush lobby of the

agency, the welcome rush of artificially cooled air reviving her somewhat.

Donna smiled brightly. "9:15," she chirped. "And you're already off to the races." Donna handed Julie three pink message slips. "And don't forget your 10:00 meeting in the conference room with Dulles Furniture," the receptionist called as her phone chimed.

Julie nodded and sighed. As usual, things were starting off with a bang. The client, Harold Dulles, would be arriving in forty-five minutes, then the agency would be making a bid via a presentation for his healthy, high-budgeted account. He had ten stores in the Washington area and he was a big media spender. It would be a good account for their shop and she'd enjoyed writing the sample copy for the presentation. She hoped they landed it.

"Tell Tess to meet me in the conference room," Julie called to Donna over her shoulder as she hurried through the lobby's double doors and into the halls of the business area. Julie tossed her briefcase and her message slips onto her neat desk. "Can't settle in now," she told herself. She just had time to grab a cup of coffee and get to the conference room ahead of Tess.

The room was quiet when Julie slipped inside. The long teak table gleamed in the dim lighting. Julie flipped the switches to a brighter intensity and scanned the grasscloth walls at Tess's storyboard art. Her friend and assistant art director had already hung the presentation for Dulles Furniture.

Julie walked from storyboard to storyboard, scanning her copy one final time. She still liked it. It was fresh and snappy. With just the right talent, it would be an eye-catching campaign on TV and billboards. They would have to choose the talent carefully, a man, definitely, tall, with an authoritative voice. "And maybe blue eyes . . . ," Julie mused distractedly.

From her position behind the desk of the law library, Julie could survey the entire room. She could observe

11

the silent stacks of books, the tables piled high with texts, and the quiet students, intense and engrossed over the thick volumes. And she could watch Paul Shannon, with little chance of his detecting her covert, adoring glances.

Julie had taken the job in the university's law library to help finance her own college education and ease her parent's financial burden. Even though she'd received a partial scholarship in English, her parents sent her money every month—money she knew strained their budget. Therefore, this job, on weekends and three nights a week, made her feel that she was helping them in some small way.

Her eyes stole over to Paul again. He sat, bent over a book, his fingers thrust through his head of thick dark brown curls. She'd watched him, silently, covertly, for months. Observed every variation of his features, every nuance of his expressions, every subtle flex of his muscles and limbs. When he stood, Julie knew he was long and lanky, lean and sinewy. He always seemed to be holding himself back, like an animal poised on the edge of bolting or an athlete tense and coiled before a race. His face was handsome, compelling, all planes and angles, highlighted by jewel-blue eyes, set slanted over strong cheekbones. She couldn't image any jury denying him anything he asked.

Julie dragged her attention from him, to check out a book for a student. She felt foolish, acting like a silly schoolgirl about Paul. But she couldn't help it. Just the sight of him made her heart pound crazily. She wondered what it would be like to be near him. How would it feel to touch his dark, curly hair. Would it be soft? Or his hands, the long slim fingers . . . what would it be like to have them touch her hair, her mouth? She blushed over her thoughts.

A glance at the wall clock told her that the library would be closing shortly. She dreaded the long walk back to her dorm in the biting cold January night. Her adjustment to the atmosphere of the sprawling New York university campus had taken her entire freshman year. She missed the safety and comfort of her sheltered life at home. She missed her family, her church, her Christian school friends. Life at the campus moved too fast. For months she'd felt off-balance and overwhelmed. But she'd survived. She studied hard, attended chapel at the campus' nondenominational services, made some friends, and kept to herself. Every summer she went back home and worked and prepared for another year of college.

She'd all but stopped dating. It was easier than wrestling every weekend with some man insensitive to her principles and values. It was a big campus, but the word did get around. "Julie Kreel doesn't put out." So, study and her job at the library filled her free time. It was enough—until that afternoon she first noticed law student Paul Shannon. From that time, her days took on an exciting purpose. Finish this day so that she could see him the next day. Or the following night. Or during the weekend. For Julie, it was purely worship from afar. He had no idea how she dreamed and fantasized about him.

She shared her secret with no one. Not even her friend and roommate, Sara. "You'll dry up and blow away," Sara often told Julie in exasperation. "You're pretty, Julie. Say the word. Pete could get you a date with any dozen of his frat brothers."

But Julie always declined. Her values were different. She didn't want to date just to avoid a lonely Saturday night. And once she saw Paul Shannon, she didn't want to date because there wasn't a single other male on campus as attractive to her as him.

The conference room door swung open and Tess Germaine entered with her usual flourish. Julie snapped her body around to greet the vivacious brunette in the lavender saucer-sized eyeglasses.

"Sorry," Tess said breezily. "Didn't mean to startle you."

Julie shrugged. "Just jittery. Don't mind me."

Tess's eyes narrowed, intuitively. "It's more than the presentation, isn't it?"

Julie leveled a look at her friend and nodded. "It would have been my sixth wedding anniversary today."

Tess shook her head and reached out to touch Julie's shoulder. The clunky jewelry on her arm rattled. "Tough. I know."

Julie believed that Tess really *did* know. Like Julie, she too was divorced. Hank Germaine had left Tess after 18 years of marriage and with two children to raise.

Tess was ten years Julie's senior, but they'd had an instant rapport from the first time they'd met when Frank Denton had hired Julie four years before as a copywriter. Tess was one of a kind . . . a thin, large-boned woman with an exaggerated sense of style that usually overwhelmed. She dressed with panache and flair, staging minor miracles with scarves and belts and department store jewelry.

From Julie's first day at work, Tess had taken her under her wing. Julie had gravitated to her, and had allowed Tess to integrate Julie into her home life, church life, the fabric of her kids' lives. It was Tess whom Julie confided in . . . Tess whom she counted as her friend. She smiled at Tess and said lightly, "Your storyboards are great. Once Van starts the presentation, Dulles doesn't stand a chance of denying us his account."

As if on cue, Van Hudson, the account executive on the project, entered the room. "All ready?" he asked. His eyes raked Julie appreciatively and she lowered her eyes to avoid his gaze. He was attractive, broad shouldered, blond, with an open, easy smile. At thirty-six he was a partner in the agency and the office grapevine heralded Van as the heir apparent when Frank Denton retired.

14

Julie stretched and strained on her tiptoes, reaching high above her head to reshelve the library book. The ladder that ran on a track above the old wooden library cases teetered and creaked beneath her weight.

"Can I do that for you?" The male voice from under the ladder caused her to jump and almost lose her precarious balance. The book slipped from her fingers and she cried out as it tumbled, bouncing off the ladder to the floor below.

"Oh!" she gasped, climbing quickly down the ladder. "I'm so sorry! Did it hit you?" She found the floor and pitched forward. Strong male hands reached out to steady her. She reeled and found herself in Paul Shannon's arms.

His blue eyes twinkled and danced and clusters of dark brown curls fell across his forehead. He smelled fresh, like soap. Julie tensed, and shrank as if to run and hide.

"You missed," he laughed. "Are you all right?"

She was speechless. To be so near him. So close, after all the months of silent adoration. Her heart pounded wildly and she could scarcely shape words into her mouth. "I—I— . . . yes. I'm fine."

He released her by degrees, his hands trailing from her shoulders to her elbows, to her hands, causing a path of warmth to linger where his fingers had traveled. She remembered her fantasies and felt her cheeks burn. What if he had read her mind?

He appraised her openly, seeing her for the first time, letting his eyes loiter along the full curve of her lips. She felt as if air had expanded her lungs and now could find no way out. She stepped back, panic filling her thoughts. Her back pressed against the hard bindings of books.

"They're about to shut this place down," Paul said with only the dusty quiet of the library surrounding them. "Could I buy you a cup of coffee?"

"I—I— have to get back to my dorm." To her own ears her voice sounded high, her answer stupid.

"Let me walk you," he offered. "Which dorm is it?"

"It—it's in the s—s—student directory," Julie stuttered,

losing all that was left of her fragile composure. She spun and hurried for the open space beyond the stacks.

"Well, what's your name?" Paul called after her.

"That's in the directory, too," she said, hitting the safety of the "Librarians Only" doorway. There she leaned weakly, for a long time waiting for her racing heart to calm and her breath to regain a steadier pace.

"Stupid! Stupid!" she admonished herself over and over. Her behavior had been childish, her actions, deranged. But to have had in secret the thoughts and desires she did about him—and then to have him materialize in the flesh and to touch her and to look at her with those blue, blue eyes. . . .

Donna delivered a tray of coffee and danish. Van reviewed the high points of his presentation while Tess, Julie, and Mel, the media buyer, listened. They were prepared when Harold Dulles swept into the room at 10:00 sharp.

Julie sipped her coffee and listened to Van's honeyed voice. Things were going very well. She admired the way Van controlled the meeting, steered the discussion, and persuaded the listening potential client. He was a dynamic man, an excellent salesman, and very urbane. Julie knew he was interested in her, but she refused and thwarted all his overtures. She'd put him off for over a year, scrupulously avoiding emotional entanglements.

Her eyes focused on Tess and her friend gave her a discreet "thumbs up." It was Tess's trademark and she'd encouraged Julie with it often. Julie was grateful that God had given her such a friend. Without Tess, she doubted she would have made it through the bouts of depression and loneliness over the past years.

Only Tess knew any of the details of Julie's brief marriage. Or of how Julie had come to this city to escape the sadness of her past. Or of how she'd taken back her maiden name in order to forget, erase the

16

pain, the sense of failure, the shame of her broken covenant.

Julie left the protection and warmth of the library. She pulled her ski cap down snugly and clutched her winter coat around her tightly. The campus was dark and cold. Drifts of snow banked the icy sidewalks. Winter in the Northeast seemed far worse than the winters back home in Ohio.

Thoughts of home made her feel lonely. She pictured her parents sitting in their family room. Dad would be watching TV. Mom would be knitting, or reading. Their thirty years of marriage was a bond of contentment and friendship that had become an unbreakable cord intertwined with love and mutual goals. A Christian marriage—founded on Christ.

"Hello, Julie," the male voice said from the darkness.

She jumped, startled, and spun to find the tall, lean body of Paul Shannon at her side. He wore a brushed leather jacket lined with fleece, worn and faded jeans, and a ski hat. A few dark errant curls poked from under the soft wool knit, giving him a boyish quality that tugged at her heart.

"B—but how did you. . . ."

He grinned and the campus streetlights caught a glimmer from his straight, white teeth. "I asked," he told her, anticipating her question. "Your name is Julie Kreel and you live in Stetson Hall West."

She colored. At the same time, her heart leaped. He'd asked about her! The thought pleased her as no other had in weeks. "And I drop books on people's heads," she added, a bit shyly.

"You can make it up to me. Have a cup of coffee with me at the Student Union."

Despite the cold, Julie felt a warm flush spread across her body. "I—I don't know," her feelings were jumbled. How could she ever look him in the eye after all she'd fantasized about him in secret?

"Don't dash my confidence," he cajoled. "I'm study-

17

ing to be a lawyer. If I can't persuade a pretty girl to have a cup of coffee with me, how will I ever make a jury believe a client is innocent?"

He smiled, dissolving her reservations. *"How, indeed?"*

"Good!" Paul said. Then he took her elbow and guided her over the slippery pathways toward the brightly lit windows of the Student Union. Inside, he brought two steaming mugs of coffee to the chipped formica-topped table where she nervously waited.

Julie felt it might all be a dream or another of her fantasies. But after fifteen minutes with Paul Shannon, his warm and open conversation, his gregarious and inviting style, she felt as if she'd known him half her life. He drew her out, a little at a time, discovering, leading, questioning her. She told him more than she'd ever told anyone, surprised at how effortless and easy it was to talk to him. An hour passed . . . and another.

"So you're an English major," he said. *"When do you graduate?"* The hum of voices, the smell of coffee and cafeteria food surrounded them. But they might have been alone on an island for all their awareness of the hubbub and activity.

"This is my last term," she said, filled with disappointment. Why had he come along now when she was ready to graduate, instead of when she'd been a sophomore or a junior? *"How about you?"*

"I've got another year in law school. Then I'll sit for the bar exams. If I pass them first try, I'll go after a job in a firm here. I've grown fond of these miserable winters," he added with a smile that lit up his eyes. *"Besides, a beginning lawyer is well paid in this state."* He paused, letting his eyes wander over her face.

She blushed and gripped her cup more tightly. The liquid had grown cold, but she didn't care. The warmth of Paul Shannon was filling her senses.

"So what are you going to do with an English degree?"

She shrugged and wrinkled her nose. *"Teach, I guess. I love creative writing. But how do you make a living at it?"*

18

Paul cocked his head, his blue eyes thoughtful. "Have you ever thought about public relations or advertising? There's good money in those fields and lots of opportunity to write."

She sat up straighter. Her eyes widened. "Why, no, I haven't," she said, rolling the suggestion around in her mind, weighing it, testing it, liking it.

"Check it out," Paul urged. "The mass communications school here is excellent. I'll bet they have a good curriculum for both fields."

Julie smiled broadly, sensing something exciting and provocative opening up. Then her features clouded. Another thought pressed into her mind. "But then I won't be able to graduate in June," she said with dismay.

He dismissed her objection. "You could take summer courses. I'll bet you could get a minor in either PR or advertising over the spring and summer terms and graduate in August. What's a couple of months?"

"Gee . . . I—I don't know." She toyed with the idea and examined the possibilities. She'd have to make arrangements with university housing for a summer term. She'd have to ask her parents for tuition money. She'd have to keep her job at the library. "Why, I'd be here all summer," she mused aloud.

Paul grinned, an easy lopsided smile that lit up his slanted, riveting eyes. "Me, too," he said, leaving no room for her to doubt if she'd ever see him again.

A warning bell went off in her subconscious. "Draw back!" it warned. "He's dangerous!" But she shut it off and listened instead to the riotous thumping of her heart.

The meeting broke up and Julie and Tess filed back to their office cubicles. "I think we got it!" Tess said, elated, at the entrance to Julie's cubbyhole.

Julie beamed her a delighted smile. "I do, too. Isn't it wonderful when everything goes right? When the presentation art doesn't slide off the walls. . . ."

"Or the slide projector doesn't jam!" Tess finished

with a laugh, both remembering other presentations that hadn't gone as well. "Got to hand it to Van," Tess continued. "He sure knows his stuff."

Julie nodded, avoiding Tess's subtle innuendo about Van's obvious interest in her. After a brief silence, Tess offered, "Hey! Why not come by for dinner tonight? Cindy's been asking about you and Rob has football practice. It'll be just us girls."

Julie agreed quickly. She really didn't want to spend the evening alone. Especially not *this* particular evening. Besides, Julie loved Tess's company. And Cindy's, too. She pictured Tess's daughter, a cute, slightly rounded 15 year old, with a heart-shaped face, green eyes, and bouncy black hair.

"Do you know what my shampoo bill is?" Tess had once wailed in exasperation. "The national debt should be so large!"

Cindy had rolled her eyes and Julie had laughed outright.

"I'd love to," Julie said now. "And Tess, thanks for asking." Her eyes softened at her friend's perception.

Julie spent the remainder of the morning creating copy on a real estate account. A rap on the wall of her cubicle caused her to start. Van Hudson leaned in and asked, "Lunch?"

Surprised, Julie glanced at her watch. So late! Why she hadn't even gone through her phone messages yet. Van appraised her warmly, his arms crossed. The glint from a solid gold watch bounced off his tanned, thick wrist.

"I don't know," Julie hedged. "I've got so much to do."

He chided her with his eyes. "I'm not pressuring you for a date, Julie. But you need to eat."

She flushed. Was she that transparent? He'd been very patient, urging but not pushing her toward a relationship. Early on, she'd told him, "I never mix my office and social life." He'd persisted. Finally, she'd said, "I only date Christians."

That had backed him off. It was true, too. After the breakup of her marriage, she vowed she'd never be out of God's will for her life again.

Van shrugged. "If you change your mind, I'll be down at the Proud Lion."

Julie nodded. She was comfortably familiar with the popular eating spot for area business people. "Thanks," she said as he walked away.

The halls of the agency were quiet. Most everyone had gone out for lunch. Julie tried to get back into the flow of her copy, but her concentration had been broken. "Rats!" she mumbled aloud.

Her phone chimed. Donna's voice greeted her. "Julie? There's a gentleman out here to see you."

"Me?" *Who in the world . . . ?*

"Julie," Donna's voice dropped, whispering. "He's *gorgeous.*"

Donna's tone caused Julie to smile. Donna was sweet, but a bit overzealous around men. Julie headed down the narrow hallway to the set of double doors that led to the plum and gray decorated lobby. She swung the doors open silently and caught sight of her visitor from the back.

Time seemed to telescope and her impressions of the next few moments moved in time-lapse photography. The man was tall and slim. The cut of his European-styled navy linen suit stretched flawlessly across his shoulders. He pivoted, effortlessly, like a spring about to uncoil. The air around him seemed charged with his controlled, animal energy. His thick dark curls, clipped and soft, accentuated the strong planes and angles of his face and the slightly slanted eyes above high cheekbones.

His blue eyes bore into her, pinning her like a moth under glass. Julie felt her color drain as she stared back, unbelieving, at Paul Shannon. Her first and only love. Her once-upon-a-time husband. Her betrayer!

CHAPTER 2

"HELLO, JULIE," THE RICH RESONANCE of his voice enveloped her. Julie felt her knees go weak. "You look as lovely as I remember."

With steeled determination, Julie tossed her hair and managed a forced, "Hello, Paul." Painfully, she realized that he was as attractive to her as he'd always been, as physically appealing as the first time she'd ever seen him. And known him. And touched him.

Neither moved. His eyes held hers magnetically, and she began to tremble. In two strides, he crossed the floor and took her hand. Her fingers had grown cold, bloodless, and she recoiled at his touch, as if he had burned her.

"You didn't get my messages?" he asked.

"I—I was busy . . ." she stammered.

"Is there someplace where we can talk?"

"The conference room . . ." Donna called from her desk, prurient curiosity all but popping out of her pores. Julie shot her a scathing look of admonishment.

Julie withdrew her hand, deliberately, and walked back through the double doors. Paul followed her into the quiet, dim interior of the conference room. She sat, cautiously, on the edge of a gray fabric chair, folding her hands neatly on top of the table to keep them from shaking.

Paul sat opposite her, filling the chair with his rangy lankiness, resting his elbow on the arm of the chair, his forefinger on his cheek. "How have you been?" he asked, never taking his eyes off her face.

Julie braced herself and took a long, shuddering breath. She stared down at her hands, clutching them so tightly that they grew numb and white. She found it difficult to look at him. Difficult to focus on the reality of his presence. Pain . . . waves of pain . . . rose of its own volition before the image of his face. *I will not let him hurt me again*, she swore silently. *Please, God, not again*. Queasiness rippled in her stomach.

"What are you doing here?" she asked stiffly.

"I've taken a job with a firm here in Washington." Her eyes flew in silent objection to meet his gaze. *No! You can't!* she silently screamed, panic-stricken.

A smile, tinged with bitterness, quirked the corner of her mouth. "It must have been quite an offer, for you to have left 'the good life' behind you."

Ignoring her barb, he said softly, "A lot has changed with me, Julie, since I last saw you."

She dragged the back of a hand across her forehead, whisking away a nonexistent tendril of hair, flinching at the agony of the images his words painted.

Her voice, controlled, finally said, "It's a big city. There was really no need for you to let me know you're living here now." She stopped, sucked in her breath, then asked, "What do you want, Paul?"

He leaned forward, his face taking on a fervent look, his words an urgent appeal. "First, I want your forgiveness." She didn't move. "Second, I want you to know I finally understand about the Kingdom of God and where I fit in it."

Her eyes narrowed and skepticism flooded through her. Sensing it, he proceeded quickly, "When God met

23

me, Julie, *really* met me, I felt such peace." His words came haltingly, as if being selective about the right ones to express the depth of his feelings. "And you know I've never been a peaceful man," he added ruefully, then continued with care, "and I know now what Christ expects from me, too."

She nodded. Oddly, she believed him. As a Christian, she knew what it meant to enter into God's presence and become a part of His body. She understood the joy and harmony that communion with Christ could bring. "I'm glad for you, Paul, but what has that to do with me—now?"

He leaned his elbows against the table, pressed the tips of his fingers together to create a pyramid. He captured her with the spellbinding intensity of his clear blue gaze. "Actually, it's stated best in Proverbs 5 . . ." he said. "The part that advises a man to 're-member the wife of his youth.' *You* are that wife, Julie. The wife I should never have let go."

Julie felt anger well within her. Waves of white-hot anger from the depths of her spirit. Her cheeks flamed, her eyes snapped, and she leaped to her feet, venomous words rising to her lips. "How dare you walk back into my life!" Her voice shook. "How dare you quote Scripture at me and expect me to . . . to. . . ." She groped for words. "To what? Paul, we're divorced! What did you expect of me? I'm glad you've got things 'right with God,' " she seethed, her voice edged with sarcasm. "But I have my own life now . . . and I don't want or need you in it! I don't want you, or your self-serving guilt feelings!"

He was on his feet and caught her arm before she reached the door. His voice was low, his eyes challenging, ignoring her outburst. "Running away again, Julie?"

She twisted free of his grasp. But his words continued, evenly, with determined thrusts. "Sooner or later, you're going to have to deal with me," he said quietly. "You can't run away forever. Not now. Not five years ago. Sooner or later, you've got to face me . . . for both our sakes," he added passionately.

Her heart brimmed with anger and bitterness. "Never!" she cried. "I will never let you near me again! You think you can come in and settled all the scores of the past with an admission of some newfound Christianity and a quote from the Bible?" Her voice had risen, but she had no control of it, no will to stop her bitter and hateful words.

"Read Mark 10, Paul! And Matthew 5!" she said hotly as she grabbed the conference room doorhandle. She stopped suddenly, feeling his piercing gaze pushing against her back. With renewed bitterness she flung cruelly over her shoulder, "or, better still, Proverbs 7!" Then Julie fled the room, as if demons from hell were pursuing her.

"What do you mean, you can't come this weekend?" Paul's voice came to her from the darkness as he held her against him under the canopy of the oak tree. The sweet loamy smell of the cool spring night surrounded them. The moon peeked intermittently between the rustling leaves, leaving moon shadows on Paul's hair and shoulders.

Julie's heart pounded and she squeezed her eyes shut against the hurt and confusion in his tone. She'd known from the first time they'd dated that it would eventually come down to this conversation. "It's not that I don't want to . . ." she began, her words coming in slow, almost painful increments. "It's just that I—I . . ." she floundered. "I just can't."

"Can't? Or won't?" he asked bitterly, letting his arms relax and fall away from her waist. A cricket sang to the night breeze. Julie stood very still, her heart pounding with confused fears. She didn't want to lose him. Oh, Lord, she didn't want to lose him!

"Julie, you're not just any girl to me. You're special to me. I want to spend the weekend with you. Sure . . . the skiing will be fun. But I want you with me." He

*pulled her close again and pressed his lips to her temple,
then down her cheek and the taut expanse of her throat.*

*A shiver of delight shot through her. She wanted him,
too! God, forgive her. But she wanted him, too. Yet, ever
since Paul's friend and roommate Ted Henderson had
first started talking about a weekend ski trip to the nearby
mountains, Julie knew what her answer would have to
be.*

*Kathy, Ted's girl, had no such convictions. She'd talked
for days about the trip, telling them about her parents'
cabin, about the free room and food, the late-spring
snow-powdered slopes, the fun they would all have together. Just Kathy and Ted. And Paul and Julie. Two
bedrooms. . . . One for each couple.*

*Paul's lips found hers and she felt as if she were melt-
ing. "Julie . . ." he whispered hoarsely. "Please . . . I
want you so bad."*

*"No," her reply was barely audible. Then, gathering
all that was left of her fragile reserve, she pushed away
from him. "I—I can't, Paul. Not like this. I won't go to
bed with you . . . because it's wrong." Her voice sounded
small and miserable. "I would never . . . I never have.
. . ." She couldn't put it into words.*

*Her cheeks burned and currents of embarrassed heat
washed over her. Paul took her by the elbows and commanded, "Julie! Look at me!"*

*Slowly, painfully, she dragged her gaze up to tangle
with his. The night breeze stirred the leaves above and
caused the moon to fall fully across his features. His
eyes were narrowed, appraising. He looked deeply into
her, ripping away the facade of her fear, laying bare the
privacy of her nature. Curiously, she saw no ridicule in
his look. Only surprise, then amazement, then
tenderness.*

*With renewed vigor, she continued, her voice stronger,
swelling with a desire to make him understand. "That
part of me is reserved, Paul. It's a one-time gift. And
because I'm a Christian, I can only give it once." Her
lifelong commitment to her God and His principles*

strengthened her further. "I'm not ashamed of what I believe," *she told him steadily.* "I will not do what is wrong for me. No matter how much I care. . . ." *Her bravery wavered.* "Even if it means losing you," *she finished, in misery.*

"Julie . . . Julie. . . ." *Paul crushed her against his chest, whispering her name again and again.* "It's me who doesn't want to lose you." *Her knees went weak and she exhaled a deep shuddering breath. She had confessed her highest principles, exposed her deepest fears, and he hadn't walked away from her! Suddenly, she felt hope surging through her.*

Paul stepped back and tilted her chin with his finger. "Hundreds of co-eds on this campus," *he clucked teasing, letting his eyes linger on her upturned face.* "And I've got to fall for the one with principles."

Julie smiled at him shyly, grateful for his understanding, his compassion, his caring. Maybe she wouldn't lose him after all! The realization caused her to hug him tightly, passionately, afraid that if she loosened her hold, he would vanish into the velvet night. She knew then that she loved Paul . . . fiercely loved him. And with a passion that transcended her five senses.

Julie hurried along the busy sidewalk, the steamy heat seeping through the soles of her feet. The brilliant, hot noonday sun beat down on her dark head, matching the heated emotions that simmered and seethed within her.

How could he? she fumed. *How could he expect to waltz back into her life as if nothing had happened. As if she might welcome him with open arms.*

Julie opened the wooden door of the Proud Lion Pub and welcomed the cool rush of air. It took a few moments for her eyes to adjust to the darkness of the interior. When they did, she glanced around the waiting area, expectantly.

"May I help you?" asked a smiling hostess.

"I—I was meeting someone," Julie wondered why she'd come here. "A Mr. Hudson," she lamely finished.

The hostess beamed. "Of course. Please follow me."

Julie fell into step behind the hostess' swaying floor-length skirt, forcing her eyes to stay on the white flounce cap the girl wore over her blond hair.

"Julie!" Her name came from the surprised lips of Van Hudson as the hostess paused in front of his table. He rose and tugged out a chair for her. "Please, sit down. I'm glad you came.' He smiled broadly, pushed aside his half-eaten salad and signaled the waiter.

"What would you like?" Embarrassed and a little ashamed of herself, she forced a bright smile and focused her full attention on his rugged, handsome features.

"Just a chef's salad." A waiter jotted down her order while Van added, "Iced tea for both of us. And hold my meal until the lady's is ready." The waiter nodded and left.

Van turned his full attention on Julie. "I'm surprised to see you—but very glad," he added, his tone taking on a warm, intimate note.

"No sense starving, is there?" she quipped valiantly, squirming under the frank open admiration of his gaze. The familiar sounds of the restaurant closed in around her and she took in the fragrance of rich foods and heady coffees.

"Well," Van started cautiously, aligning his silverware on the red tablecloth, "as long as I'm on a roll . . . how about going out with me for dinner?"

Julie sucked in her breath. What had she expected? She'd all but run into his arms. *Paul! Darn you anyway.* Why did he have to come back into her life? Why, when she was finally getting herself back together again? Why, when everything they'd once shared was gone. Buried . . . beneath a blanket of rejection and deception.

"Tonight?" Van asked, his cool eyes bright and anticipating.

"I have plans tonight," she hedged, remembering Tess.

"Saturday?" he persisted.

She wavered. *Why not?* "Next Saturday."

"A whole week?" he asked, dismay evident in his voice.

She opened her mouth to speak. But he raised his hand to stop her words. "Sorry. If the lady wants to wait a week, that's fine with me. After all," he added, looking carefully into her eyes, "I've waited a year already. What's another week?"

Julie blushed. Had she really put him off that long? Van had joined the agency, bringing fresh vitality, filled with ideas, plans, and vigor. He'd garnered several new accounts, solidified some old ones, and brought new excitement and vision to the business' ranks.

I should be dating! Julie told herself firmly through the clink of china and silverware. Van was dynamic, handsome, interesting, and persistent. She'd sat around too long, hiding herself from the world. Afraid of making emotional commitments. Afraid of letting her feelings out.

"Well, no more!" she told herself hotly. The past was dead. And Paul Shannon could go hang! Julie was through running away. Despite Paul's accusation, she'd already dealt with him. She'd divorced him five years before! She turned her fullest smile, her loveliest expression, on Van. He arched an eyebrow and toasted her with his water goblet.

"To Saturday night," he said, allowing his voice to caress the words and Julie's mind to decipher his intimate and hopeful intent.

Julie returned home from work, gathered her mail, fed Hector, changed into jeans and a print blouse, and headed over to Tess's place for supper. The daylight lingered as she drove through the quiet streets of Georgetown, the coolness of approaching evening reviving her spirits.

With sparse traffic, it didn't take long to make the journey from her apartment complex in Arlington to Tess's brownstone. The address was impressive. Georgetown seemed to be the gathering place for Washington's social elite, for senators, diplomats, and embassy people.

Julie had asked Tess once about her choice of address. "When Hank walked out, I couldn't stand the thought of staying in that gargantuan museum of a home. I wanted a place that was mine. With no memories of Hank Germaine. And I wanted the kids to have something more . . . since they no longer had a father," she'd said, her words edged with bitterness. "So, I bought this place. Hank paid for it . . . kicking and screaming, but he owed us." Her eyes had grown hard as the old, unpleasant memories swept back.

Julie slipped her sports car into a spot near the yellow facade of Tess's home and jogged up the cobbled steps to the front door. A window box, brimming with chrysanthemums, encircled a white-trimmed bay window. She rang the bell. Cindy pulled open the door with a squeal.

"Julie!" the pert teen cried, tossing her arms around Julie and pulling her inside. "It's the greatest—Mom's fixing Chinese. I can't wait to tell you all the awesome news!" Julie smiled. Cindy Germaine spoke only in superlatives. For her, life was either "fabulous" or "gross." There was no in-between.

Cindy was special to Julie. Maybe because she reminded her so much of herself at that age. A wide-eyed innocent whose most complex problems consisted of what sweater to wear to school.

Cindy dragged her down the hall, into the kitchen where Tess stood over a steaming wok, tossing vegetables and meat chunks around with a spatula. "Glad you're here!" Tess called. "Fix Julie some iced tea, Cindy." Julie leaned across the counter and inhaled the spicy aromas of soy sauce and ginger.

"Yum . . . I'm starved."

They sat together at Tess's lacquered dining room table and enjoyed the meal, letting their conversation rise and fall in animated eddys.

"So how's school this year?" Julie asked Cindy, who had just entered tenth grade and her first year of high school.

Cindy wrinkled her nose and picked up a piece of meat with her chopsticks. "Algebra is the pits. I can hack English. The senior guys are stuck-up."

Julie recoiled in mock-horror. "*All* the senior guys? How awful!"

Cindy blushed. "Well . . . maybe a couple are okay."

Tess interrupted, "Like Jud Ellis."

"Mother!"

"Ellis? Ellis?" Julie mulled over the name. "Why, isn't he in the youth group at church with you?" She recalled a wide-shouldered youth with brown hair and brown eyes. He was a handsome boy, certainly capable of setting any teen girl's heart aflutter.

"The Ellises go to our church," Tess confirmed. "Jud is Mr. Macho." Cindy shot her mother a pouting look. "He and Rob are on the football team together. Jud's pretty good about attending youth group. I'm hoping he'll be a positive influence on Rob."

The concerned look on Tess's face as she mentioned her son caused Julie to sober. She knew that Tess was worried about 16-year-old Rob. Unlike Cindy, he was a loner and rebellious, with a sizable chip on his shoulder. "He needs a father," Tess had often lamented. "More than Cindy even, he needs a strong male figure in his life. I pray for him constantly. For me, too," she'd admitted ruefully. "That we'll both survive his teens!"

"How is the youth group?" Julie asked.

Cindy perked immediately. "I love it! The Freytags are the best leaders ever!" Julie nodded, remembering the couple fondly. Mary and Don Freytag had acted as youth leaders for the past three years and were loved and adored by the teen group that attended and participated in their community and church serving activities.

"When's her baby due?" Julie asked.

"January," Cindy said. "The youth group's gonna have a shower for her. Do you want to come?"

"When?" Julie asked, mentally calculating that Mary was barely five months along.

"Oh, months and months from now."

Julie laughed. "Then ask me again 'months and months' from now."

The jangle of the phone caused Cindy to leap to her feet. "I'll get it. It's probably Tina."

"Again?" Tess rolled her eyes. "You just talked to Tina."

"Well we have to decide what we're wearing tomorrow," she said, acting as if her mother had just emerged from the Dark Ages.

"How could I have wondered?" Tess teased as her daughter bounded out of the room.

Silence settled over the room after Cindy's exit. Both women sat as the warmth of the conversation, the effects of the meal, and the depths of their friendship embraced them.

Tess poured Julie another cup of green tea and Julie smiled her thanks. "So," Tess began, eyeing Julie over the rim of her cup, "when are you going to tell me about what happened today in the office? And about that 'gorgeous' man who made you run out of the place like a rabbit, according to Donna?"

The noonday encounter with Paul came back in a flood. Julie sighed deeply and set her cup down on the table's gleaming black surface. "Paul's back," she told her friend simply.

"I wondered as much," Tess pushed her lavender-tinted glasses up on her nose. "Couldn't think of anybody else who could affect you like that. Except maybe the devil himself." She smiled, encouraging Julie to wipe the frown off her pretty face.

Suddenly, with vehemence, Julie pounded the table

32

with a tightly balled fist. "Why?" she demanded. "Why would he come now? After five years? And why would he move here in the first place?"

Tess shrugged. "What did he tell you?"

"Just that he'd taken a job with a firm in Washington. Oh, and he also said that he'd finally found God after all this time." Her tone reflected her incredulity.

"You don't believe him?"

"Too little, too late," Julie said, her voice flat with bitterness.

"But it's good that he's a Christian. . . ."

Julie shrugged. "He's always been a Christian. Just not . . . not. . . ." She struggled to put her impressions into words. "Paul loves 'the good life,' Tess. Money, prestige, the 'right' job with the 'right' law firm. That was always more important to him than anything. Even me. . . ." She swallowed the dregs of her memories.

"So maybe he's changed. A right relationship with God can do that, you know." She nudged Julie's arm. "It *can*," she added as skepticism crossed Julie's face.

"Don't think me uncharitable," Julie told Tess, tossing her dark hair from her shoulders. "I'm glad Paul's discovered a deeper relationship with God. We certainly had our share of discussions about it. But what does he expect from me? To welcome him back with open arms? To pat him on the head and say, 'Gee, Paul, good for you'? We're divorced and he's out of my life." Her anger had welled and her breath came in sharp gasps by the end of her speech.

Tess eyed her, unwilling to comment. "So you took off like a scared bunny," she said, changing the direction of the conversation.

"And that's another thing Paul made me do!" Julie snapped, remembering her impetuous flight to Van. "I was so flustered I ran right to Van Hudson and accepted a date with him."

Tess clapped ceremoniously. "It's about time! You've kept that guy dangling for a year. I'm surprised he's still asking!"

"But, Tess, I don't really want to date anyone."

"Why?" Tess asked, tapping her long fingernails against the tabletop. "Julie, you're 27 years old. You have a whole life ahead of you. Don't throw the baby out with the bath water," she urged. "Don't judge all men by what happened between you and Paul." She paused, then gathering her forces, plunged ahead. "And don't judge Paul by his past. If he's been born again, he's a new creature. A different man from the one you knew. Maybe you should try to get to know him again."

"Never!" Julie cried, leaping to her feet. She began clearing the table with concentrated fury. "I loved him, Tess. More than anything in the world, I loved him. And he almost destroyed me."

She swept from the room, laden with plates. Tess sighed and rose to follow her into the kitchen.

Julie found it difficult to concentrate on the textbook with Paul sitting next to her in the soft green grass. The letters kept squiggling in front of her eyes and the warmth from his thigh, pressed against her leg as he sat cross-legged next to her, made her aware of his masculine presence. Too aware.

A breeze, heavy with the scents of summer, ruffled the pages of her open book. Every time she glanced sideways at Paul, she envied the breeze fluttering the clusters of curls on his forehead. Her fingers longed to reach over and touch their softness.

It was cool under the tree where they'd spread their books to study, and flickering shadows danced and played with sunlight on the white pages of her book. Julie had insisted that they study outside in the quiet heat of the summer morning on the campus. Paul had wanted to study with her in his apartment. Ted and Kathy had gone away for the weekend, but Julie knew she didn't dare study with him at his place. The temptations of being alone with him were too great. Too real.

Julie found it increasingly difficult to back away from his kisses, his caresses, his soft and tender words. And it unnerved her. In the several months they'd dated, Paul had been gentle, loving, caring. He never urged her beyond the limit she'd set on their physical relationship. But she wanted him to. She wanted him more than ever. Especially now that the summer term was drawing to a close.

Julie had almost completed her advertising courses. In three weeks she would be graduating. Paul still had another year of law school. She was torn. Should she go back home? Should she look for a job and stay near the campus? Or go for campus job counseling and try for a job in another city far away? The indecision gnawed at her daily.

"I think I have a solution to our problem," Paul's voice caused her to start. He was looking at her, intently, from the depths of his clear, blue eyes.

"What problem?" she asked, surprised, now realizing that he'd been observing her, silently, all morning.

"You know . . ." he said sheepishly. "Our sex problem."

Her mouth dropped in open surprise. "What 'sex problem'? We're not having sex."

"I know," he said drily. "That's the problem."

Julie giggled aloud and poked him with her pencil. "Is that all you ever think about?"

"Of course not," his boyish grin endeared him to her even more. His eyes grew serious as did his voice. "I think about how much I'll miss you when we're not together all the time."

Something caught in her throat. "Me, too."

He placed his hand behind her neck and pulled her toward him, until their foreheads touched. "Julie . . . Julie. . . ." They sat quietly for a moment, the sounds of summer surrounding their togetherness. A butterfly fluttered between them, causing them both to push back with a laugh.

"So what's your solution to our problem?" she asked, forcing more lightness into her voice than she felt.

"We can get married," he told her softly.

For a stunned moment she sat perfectly still. "W—what?"

"Married," he restated. Then his face grew animated and his voice intense and persuasive. "I love you, Julie. I don't want things to end between us just because you're graduating."

"But—but you still have another year of law school," she offered, not daring to hope he'd truly asked her to marry him.

"Yes, I know. It would have been a lot more convenient if we'd met next year. But we didn't." He took her hand in his and laced his long fingers through hers. "You're everything I want in a woman. I love you and I want you to marry me."

Julie's heart soared and she could scarcely catch her breath. Marry Paul Shannon! The universe was at her fingertips! "But where will we live? How . . . ?"

He silenced her by placing his hand lightly against her mouth. "Shh-shh," he commanded, staring into the core of her heart. "Details. Everything else is details." With measured conviction, he added, "This is the most important case I'll ever plead, Julie. Don't say 'no.' "

"How soon?"

"Could your family get a wedding together by mid-September? That way, I could start my last year in law school as a married man. And maybe . . ." he said, chucking her gently under the chin, "maybe, I could get some serious studying done instead of thinking about you all the time."

She slid into his arms, holding him tight, her embrace giving him her answer. In six weeks she'd be Mrs. Paul Shannon! Her life cup was filled to overflowing. And nothing under God's sun could rob her of this exquisite joy! Nothing!

CHAPTER 3

JULIE SLIPPED INTO THE PEW of the packed church as silently and as unobtrusively as possible. She hated to be late. But she hadn't slept well the night before. She'd tossed and turned for hours, finding sleep only as dawn was about to break and had slept far past her usual Sunday morning arousal hour. But she couldn't forget that Paul had walked back into her life. Paul, handsome and virile and electric. And she resented him deeply for it.

They were divorced. That chapter of her life was over forever. Why had he come back to haunt her after five years? Why? Julie rubbed her hand across her forehead and tried to pick up the thread of the liturgy from the assistant pastor at the pulpit in the front of the church. "Help me get it together, Lord," she prayed silently. "Help me to concentrate on You today. Give me Your peace."

The church always gave her comfort, with its beautiful stained-glass windows and rubbed oak pews and cool stone walls. It was a magnificent church, a wonderful dwelling place for the Spirit of God. The music of the pipe organ filled the building, and prisms of rainbow light danced off the stone altar through the circular multicolored window set high above the rafters. The main pulpit was positioned to the left, high and jutting out over the pews.

The organ played the strains of a favorite hymn and Julie flipped through the hymnal to blend her light soprano voice into the tide of voices surrounding her. The church was very crowded, but from where she stood she could see the back of Tess's head along with Cindy's and Rob's. The 16-year-old boy stood three inches taller than his mother, yet even from the back Julie could see the squared, rebellious set of his broad shoulders. Julie sighed. Poor Tess. She'd probably dragged Rob to the service this morning.

The hymn ended and the congregation sat down in a rustle of Sunday clothing and waited expectantly as David Wilson strode forward, his robes flowing behind him, to the richly carved pulpit where he would preach. Julie leaned forward slightly, eager to hear every word spoken by this minister, this tall, young, handsome, and vibrant man of God.

David Wilson had been at the church for only a year, and already he'd doubled attendance and tripled the Sunday morning service schedule. The church was jammed with people for every service, revitalized by this zealous young minister. He'd certainly made a difference in Julie's life! His messages had opened up the Bible for her with truths she'd never seen and lessons about Christian life she'd never heard.

"Good morning!" David said. The entire congregation nodded at him in unison. He raised his light brown eyes from his notes and swept the congregation with one long and commanding look.

"One announcement," David's rich melodious voice rose and echoed off the church's stone interior. "The youth group will meet for a swim party at the Freytag's today at four. Sharon, myself, and our kids will be there, too, so all you young people come over. We've got a lot of plans to set for the upcoming holiday season."

Julie's eyes automatically fell on the face of Sharon Wilson, seated in the choir behind the free-standing altar. What a striking woman! With soft blond hair and radiant smiles, she was a portrait of composure and serenity. Her beauty seemed to flow from the inside out, spilling out of her eyes in warm glances at the people whom David served.

Julie also saw Tess whisper something into Rob's ear and watched as the boy jerked aside and twisted his shoulders defiantly. Cindy stared straight ahead, ignoring her brother's rude movement. Julie whispered another silent prayer on her friend's behalf.

David began his sermon and Julie let his message wash and flow over her like waters of renewal. She *needed* his sermon today. More than ever, Julie needed to hear how much God cared about her. She needed to understand His purposes for her life. His reasons for turning her world upside down after all this time. . . .

"Mom, I'm so nervous I think I'm sick to my stomach!" Julie said in the privacy of her bedroom.

"All brides are nervous, honey," Ruth assured her daughter, smoothing out the trailing skirt of the magnificent white wedding dress Julie wore. Her firm, sure touches comforted Julie somewhat, but she found standing still difficult while her mother fastened the row of pearl buttons down her back.

"I can't believe I'll be Mrs. Paul Shannon in an hour," Julie said to her reflection in the mirror of her dresser. More butterflies fluttered in her stomach, half with excitement for the ceremony ahead and half for the anticipation of her wedding night. This very night Paul would make love to her. This very night she would know the wonder of his body. The delight of belonging to him completely. She shivered at the thought. Of her own willingness, her unreserved abandon.

"Are you cold?" Ruth asked. *"You're shivering."*

Julie blushed. "Not one bit. Thanks, Mom," she added with genuine love for her mother's presence. "Thanks to you and Dad for getting this wedding together on such short notice."

"Honey, it was our joy, believe me," Ruth completed her task and straightened to look lovingly at Julie.

"I mean getting everything organized the way you have in just four weeks. Well, I'll never forget how much you've done."

"Marriage is forever, Julie," Ruth commented. "If Paul's the man God has chosen for you, the least your dad and I can do is help you two get off to the best possible start."

"If." Her mother had said "if." Not "since" or "because." A slight uneasiness stirred inside Julie.

"You do approve of Paul?" she asked, suddenly hesitant and wary.

Ruth dropped her eyes and clasped Julie's hand. "Of course, I do!"

"No, Mom, there's something you're not saying. I can feel it."

"Paul is handsome, engaging, ambitious," Ruth began lightly. "And you're head over heels in love with him, Julie. A blind person could see it."

"But. . . ." Julie added the unspoken word to the end of Ruth's sentence.

"Your father and I love you very much and want only the best for you. We want you to always remember that you belong to God first and to the world second," Ruth said cautiously.

"Paul's a Christian, Mother," Julie inserted, sensing Ruth's direction. "I'd never marry a man who wasn't a Christian!" She and Paul had discussed it before she'd even brought him home to meet her family.

"Me?" he'd teased, gently kissing the tip of her nose. "Why I'm an old choirboy from way back."

"I know he's a Christian, Julie," Ruth said, striving to mollify her daughter's irritation. "Honey," she asked, *turning her conversation in a new direction. "Have you ever heard the term 'Sunday Christian?' "*

"Yes."

"Sometimes we Christians become 'Sunday only' people. But Christianity is an everyday thing. It's a way of life, not just a once-a-week activity."

Julie gasped. "Is that what you think about Paul? That he's a Christian in name only?"

"It doesn't matter what I think, Julie. It matters what God thinks. I brought it up because I love you and I don't want your spiritual life to suffer because of split loyalties between your husband and your life in God. Paul is a very ambitious man," she cautioned. "He—he may not have all his priorities in order."

Julie blinked, incredulous at her mother's thoughts and words. Her parents had met Paul only days before. They'd talked to each other at length and Paul was his typical charming, winsome self. Yet Ruth had detected something beneath his surface that Julie had never seen, never encountered about his basic nature. Julie wanted to be offended. She wanted to be angry. But she could not. Because she knew Ruth was a wise and good woman with a firm and unwavering loyalty to God. And she'd been married for thirty years. She knew what it meant to be a Christian wife!

Instead, she swallowed and said, "I love Paul so much it hurts. But I'll never turn away from God. Never!"

"It never occurred to me that you would, Julie. You belong to Him. I'm sure of that. Frankly, Paul needs you in his life. He needs the dedication to God that you have. You can't make that happen for him. Only God can. But support him. Pray for him. There's so much more to being a wife than fixing meals and cleaning house. It's loving, Julie. Loving and supporting and serving and praying for your husband. There's no other way."

Julie gathered her mother in her arms and hugged her tightly. She would do as her mother had counseled. She would be there for Paul always. Always! Because she loved Paul. Because she loved God.

This day she was moving from the world of singleness into the world of marriage. A world of the sacred covenant, ordained by God. She would leave her father and mother and "cleave" to her husband. And together they would become one flesh all the days of their lives.

Julie joined the throng of people who flowed down the aisle of the church after the service and David's inspiring message. She tried to catch Tess's eye, but the crush of people was too great, so she moved slowly toward the doors and the outer steps where David stood greeting his parishioners.

"Great message!" she heard from the people around her. Julie spotted Mary Freytag and her eyes dropped to the slight bulge beneath her bright red maternity dress. Don slipped his arm protectively around his wife's shoulders and shielded her from the shuffling, bumping motions of the crowd.

Julie reached the doorway and David Wilson grasped her hand warmly. "Julie! How good to see you." His brown eyes danced and Julie responded to the kindness and intuitive searching of their depths. "I missed you in Bible class today."

She shrugged. "Sorry. I overslept." A blush crept into her cheeks as his thoughtful gaze bore into her.

"My office is always open," he reminded her softly.

She nodded, unable to meet his eyes again and hurried down the stone steps to the sidewalk below. How did he know she was hurting? How could he possibly know by just looking at her? Was she so transparent?

Julie smiled at a few other members and waited for Tess to emerge through the church doors. She tapped her toe impatiently and casually looked to her left. She saw him at once. Paul Shannon stood less than ten feet away, staring straight at her with obvious surprise.

His eyes were the color of star sapphires in the brilliant morning sunlight. The cut of his blue suit emphasized his lean, hard elegance. She drew a sharp breath and turned, walking as quickly as possible through the milling people to the parking lot. Why was he here? Was there no place in Washington where she could be free of him?

Julie arrived, breathless, at her car and grabbed the doorhandle. Her stomach fluttered and her breath came in short gasps. "I have to get out of here," she told herself. But her flight was halted in mid-movement when Paul's strong, slim fingers curled over hers on the car door.

"Julie! Wait!" he commanded. She whirled and faced him. He towered above her, his body inches from hers. Her back was pressed into the side of the car. In effect, she was pinned—as helpless to flee as an insect trapped between a screen and a window glass.

"Leave me alone!"

His hands found her shoulders and his firm hold made her stand erect and still in front of him. The imprint of his fingers burned through the cotton voile of her dress.

"Julie! Stop this running!" His eyes reinforced the command. She stopped struggling and eyed him defiantly, tilting her chin upward in arrogant indignation.

"What are you doing here?" she demanded, trying to make her voice cold and hard. "This is *my* church."

Paul arched a dark eyebrow over his cool blue eyes. "*Your* church? I'm sorry, Julie. I didn't see your name engraved on the door when I arrived this morning."

She blushed furiously and felt her facade of composure and disdain crumble. "That's not what I meant!"

"I came," Paul interrupted, "because everyone I asked recommended this church as alive and on fire. I came to hear David Wilson preach. I came because it's Sunday morning and I wanted to go to church."

"It was never important to you before!" she snapped, then regretted her sharp words when his face clouded.

He dug his fingers into her shoulders again. "Come with me." He pulled her forward and propelled her

43

across the parking lot to a sleek black Ferrari parked under a tree. A group of teenage boys from the congregation parted from the sides of the car at their approach. Julie saw Rob in the group admiring the car.

"Let go of me!" she demanded, then gasped at the automobile as he pulled open the door. "Is this yours?" she asked, her pique momentarily forgotten by the sight of the expensive car.

"All mine," he said tersely. "Get in."

The cluster of boys looked on with great curiosity.

"I will not!"

"Get in!" he said again, his voice and eyes hard with controlled anger. She still hung back. Finally, he said, "If you don't get in, Julie, I will put you in. And wouldn't that cause a sensation here in the church parking lot?"

"You wouldn't dare."

"Try me."

She believed him.

"You-uh-you okay, Julie?" Rob asked, eyeing Paul suspiciously. Jud Ellis closed in next to Rob.

Oh, dear Lord! Julie thought. *I can't cause a scene.* "It—it's all right, Rob," she assured Tess's son, his gesture of gallantry touching her. "Really. I—I know Mr. Shannon from my college days."

Paul nodded toward the youths, his mouth set in a grim line. He secured Julie firmly inside the car, walked to the opposite side, and slid behind the wheel.

"Where are we going?" she demanded as the powerful engine roared to life. "You can't just drive off with me! What about my car?"

"We're going to talk," Paul announced firmly. "Someplace quiet with no distractions. We're going to get some things settled once and for all. I'll bring you back to your car later."

Words of protest sprang to Julie's lips. But they died there as she saw the hard set of his clenched jaw. The purring black machine glided onto the road, took a few curves, and slipped into the flow of Beltway traffic. Paul shifted expertly from gear to gear and the machine responded like a lover to his commands.

Julie sank back against the black leather upholstery with a sigh. Like it or not, she was going where Paul Shannon wanted to take her. Like it or not, he was back in her life once again.

Julie bounded up the worn steps of the old brownstone apartment building, bubbling with excitement, overflowing with joy. She'd gotten the job! It was hers! She was a full-fledged copywriter. A fulltime employee at her first job out of college. The salary wasn't spectacular, but she and Paul had already figured that if she could land this job and keep her weekend job at the law library, then he could finish law school without having to work.

The director of the law school had asked Paul to assist a professor by teaching some labs to new fall law school arrivals, and that, coupled with Julie's income, meant that Mr. and Mrs. Paul Shannon could live very nicely. Far better, in fact, than most of the financially struggling married students. Some held down three and even four jobs, trying to pay bills and finish school.

She couldn't wait to get inside their tiny apartment and throw herself into Paul's arms. He'd sounded so pleased when she'd called and told him after her interview. "I knew you could do it, baby!" he'd said into the receiver. "Now hurry home and we'll celebrate!"

She caught the bus and arrived just before six o'clock. She inserted her key into the old lock and jiggled it. It swung open and the delicious aroma of sizzling steaks greeted her nose.

"Paul!" she gasped as he emerged from the kitchen, a fork in one hand, an old towel tied rakishly around his hips. "What are you doing?"

"Why, cooking my woman the best meal ever!" He crossed the room and kissed her quickly on the mouth. "Gotta get back to the steaks," he mumbled, "but hold that pose."

She kicked off her shoes and padded after him, her eyes taking in all his preparations for her arrival. Their simple round wooden table was set with the two place settings of the good china they'd received a week before as a wedding gift. A pale ivory linen cloth covered the table and trailed onto the floor, woefully long for the tiny top. Two candles, set comically in crystal bud vases, flickered in the dimly lit room.

"Oh, Paul," she sighed, tears of love springing to her eyes. "It's beautiful. . . ."

She watched him bend over the oven door in the shoe-box-sized kitchen and stab the steaks. "Rare, madame?" he asked.

"Rare," she confirmed, a double meaning in her response.

"You go sit down," he ordered. "This is your night."

She obeyed and in a few minutes he brought the meat, two baked potatoes, and a salad to the table. He served her, then sat across from her, his long legs barely able to fit under the table.

Her heart swelled with renewed love for him. The tantalizing smell of the food caused her mouth to water in anticipation. Paul raised his goblet and toasted, "To the beautiful, exciting, and soon to be rich, Mrs. Paul Shannon."

She laughed, the mirth bubbling within her like a fountain. "You're crazy! But I still love you." She looked at his dancing blue eyes and the clusters of thick curls that framed his angular face. "But steak. We won't be rich for long, Paul Shannon. Why, I'll bet you blew an entire week's grocery budget on this meal," she chided, her tone teasing and light.

"So, we'll eat hot dogs for the rest of the week." His eyes burned in the flickering glow of the candles and Julie felt her blood running hot under his gaze. Her pulse quickened and she couldn't tear her eyes away from his lingering look. "You're worth it," his voice said huskily.

He stood, pushing his chair back and crossed to her.

The food grew cold and forgotten. The candles burned low and shapeless. The china sat gleaming and waiting long after they had left the room. . . .

"Nice car," Julie said, an undercurrent of sarcasm threading her words.

"Thanks."

"But you always did like the finer things of life," she added, feeling angry and helpless over his ability to still affect her.

"I have little else to spend my money on," he countered tightly, never letting his eyes off the road. "No family, you know."

Hot words sprang to her lips, but she forced them back. Snide remarks weren't going to get them anyplace. Julie let out a long controlled sigh and asked, "All right, Paul. Truce. I don't want to have a battle royal with you. What do you want? Why did you practically kidnap me out of the church parking lot?"

He exhaled a long breath, and she saw the tension leave the rigid set of his jaw and hands. "I honestly didn't know you attended that church, Julie. I went there because I'd heard about David Wilson and I wanted to hear him preach. Frankly, I'm glad I did. He's a powerful preacher."

She didn't respond, so he continued, "And I'm going back to hear him next Sunday."

Julie stirred, opening her mouth to protest. "I'm in Washington for my own reasons, Julie," he continued. "I'm not persecuting you. Or following you. Or haunting you. I got your message five years ago about how you felt about me."

Angry words again leaped up to her throat, but he cut her off. "I think it's a big enough town for us to coexist in, don't you?" He turned the full force of his blue eyes on her and her pulse raced in spite of herself.

"Perhaps you're right. We don't have any say-so in each other's lives now, do we?" Her tone was cool and she hoped final about future contact between them.

47

She would force herself to see him once a week at church. The Lord would see her through every encounter.

Paul downshifted the car and glided it alongside a curb. "Let's walk." He came around and opened her door and helped her out of the low-slung automobile. She took his hand only long enough to regain her balance, dropping it like a hot coal as soon as she had her footing.

Julie looked around. Surprised, she saw he'd parked near the Lincoln Monument. "Let's go in," Paul said. "It's hot out here. Besides, I always liked Mr. Lincoln."

The afternoon heat beat down on Julie as she hurried up the pale carved stone steps next to Paul. Her heels made a clicking sound and she arrived, breathless, in the giant rotunda of the vast monument. Coolness seeped from the marble as she gazed up at the massive white statue of Abe Lincoln seated in a chair. She felt dwarfed by the marble presence. Except for an elderly couple, they were alone.

" 'When in the course of human events . . .' " Paul read the familiar words from the wall. "That's what we were, Julie. A human event."

"The past is the past," she said, trying to believe the trite words she uttered. "You're right. Washington is a big city. Except for church, we'll travel in completely different circles."

From the corner of her eye, Julie watched Paul gazing up at the enormous statue. His brow was knit thoughtfully, his hands thrust deep in his trouser pockets. "I know I threw you a curve turning up in your office. I'm sorry. But I wanted you to know I was in town." Paul turned then and looked down at her and without warning, her insides went mushy. *Why? Why?* she wondered in frustration.

He said, "I always end up hurting you, don't I?" A rueful smile played across his tantalizing mouth. "It's taken me years, Julie. Too many years . . . but I finally see my life in a new perspective. A life in Christ isn't some abstract goal like the 'right' job or an expensive car. It's a relationship, communion with His Spirit, a oneness with His image. Growing up into His fullness can't be earned. It has to be granted step by step, by faith, by grace. And sometimes, it's painful." His voice grew hushed, subdued.

She nodded, not trusting her voice to respond.

He continued, "I wish I'd known then what I know now. I wish I'd known God then the way I do now. Things might have ended differently."

"Hey, get up. You promised you'd go to church with me this morning. . . ." Julie tugged the covers from her husband's sleeping form. He lay on his stomach, the long, sinewy expanse of his back exposed to her.

"Go away," he groaned. His dark curls were rumpled and pressed against the stark white of the pillow. "Give me a break, Julie. I studied until 2 a.m."

She felt frustration bubble up. It was always like this. Every Sunday morning. Julie always went to the campus chapel alone while Paul slept. Once home from the service, she had to eat a quick lunch and get ready for her job at the law library. They had less and less time together. She'd looked forward to spending the Sunday morning hour with Paul in church. Together. They had so little "togetherness" with their hectic schedules. It ate at her.

"But you promised . . ." she urged, poking him with her finger.

"Next Sunday," he mumbled as he drifted back into sleep.

She stared at him, anger, confusion, frustration warring for undivided attention inside her. Finally, she let out a long sigh and said, "Sure . . . next time. . . ." He didn't hear her. He'd already fallen back to sleep.

"Paul," Julie said slowly, choosing her words carefully, unmindful of Lincoln staring down at them. "I— I wish there was something I could say. I don't know what you want from me, but I want as little contact as possible between us. I didn't marry you lightly. I didn't divorce you lightly. It—it still hurts." Tears pricked at the back of her eyes.

He kept his hands in his pockets. "I'm sorry for what I did to you, Julie." Vivid memories threatened to surface, and Julie struggled to keep them away. She couldn't remember *that* day now! She'd spent too many years trying to forget *that* horrible day when her world had ended. . . . His rich voice cut through her thoughts. "I loved you very much, Julie. I never wanted to hurt you like that."

The tears threatened to spill over. What was she to believe? His words, his confession of new values sounded so sincere and honest. But she wouldn't allow him to deceive her again. Never! "Take me back to the church parking lot, Paul. Please!" She turned abruptly and headed out of the monument, down the mountain of steps, toward his car. Her anger was completely gone. All that was left was sadness. Incredible, heart-rending sadness. A sadness born of betrayal, of something forever lost, never to be regained.

CHAPTER 4

JULIE WAS NERVOUS. Van Hudson was arriving for their date in fifteen minutes and she was as fidgety and nervous as a schoolgirl going to her first prom. She scrutinized herself in the mirror for the hundredth time and found that she looked all right on the outside. But on the inside she was a quivering mass of jelly. Tess had called earlier to say, "Good luck and have a ball!" Julie wished she was more appreciative of Van's interest. But she wasn't.

In the first place, she didn't really want to go. But she'd promised. And Van's parting words to her Friday after work had been, "We'll do the town. Beautiful. First, the play at the Kennedy Center, then a quiet late supper at my club in Georgetown." His blue eyes twinkled and roamed her with obvious anticipation.

She'd smiled—more cheerful than she felt and said, "Till tomorrow night."

In the second place, this was the first serious date she'd had in years. "Too many years," she told her reflection with dogged determination. She'd chosen a mauve-colored crepe silk dress that gathered at her waist and fell in folds to her knees. A mandarin collar with a diamond shaped opening at the throat revealed pale white skin beneath the stunning fabric. The color complimented her thick dark hair and wide brown eyes. She still felt like she was playing dress-up as she slipped mauve satin sandals on her feet.

Just then, the doorbell rang. Julie inhaled with a start, forced a bright smile on her lips and went to the door to meet Van. He looked striking in a black suit with an ivory-colored silk shirt, and he gave a low appreciative whistle to the slim woman in front of him. "You remind me of a delicious, ripe plum," he mused. She blushed at his word choice and took his hand.

The evening air had cooled, bringing the promise of autumn to the city. Julie concentrated on being attentive, cheerful, and chatty during the ride to the Performing Arts Center. Yet she was grateful for the distraction of the play and felt the pressure to be companionable lift by the third act.

Later, at his private supper club, they dined on shrimp tempura, broiled pompano and Caesar salad in a room graced by a mixture of rich old woods, pewter, and brick. The tables, draped in pale blue linen, were partitioned off into private booths. The area, subtly lit by glowing candles, encased them in a private, intimate world of crystal and warmth, of quiet music and flickering light.

Several times, Van took her hand across the table, clasped it tightly, and gazed deeply into her eyes. As they stood to leave, he held her wrap and when she slid into the sleeves, his arms tightened around her shoulders.

The contact unnerved her. Not because she was attracted to him. But because he just didn't feel "right." He was shorter than Paul, broader across the shoulders. The scent of him was unfamiliar, the touch of his hands strange. She chastised herself, *Van likes you. He's a terrific man. He's handsome and fun. What's the matter with you?*

"Julie," he said her name, softly in her ear. His breath fluttered her hair and caused a shiver to travel along the length of her back. But the cadence wasn't right, the rhythm all wrong.

"Yes?" she answered, stiffly.

"Just, Julie," he said. "You are so lovely. I want to do this again. I want to see you as much as possible."

Her muscles tensed. *I haven't given him half a chance,* she told herself. *One date doesn't constitute a fair trial.* . . . "Of course," she said, forcing unfelt enthusiasm in her voice.

His arm tightened on her back and she tensed, reflexively. *Too much, too soon,* she said inwardly.

Back at her apartment, she unlocked the door, then stood, awkwardly, twisting the braid of her evening bag in her hands. He wanted to come in. It was written in his eyes. But she didn't want that. She wasn't ready to deal with more than a date at this point.

Van's blue eyes—*pale blue, like summer sky, not dark blue, like sapphires*—expressed their disappointment. But he didn't press her. He did say, "There's something I've been wanting to do for over a year, Julie." His husky voice left no doubt in her mind as to his intention. Van lifted her chin and lowered his mouth to hers. His kiss was warm and ardent. It, too, was all wrong. The texture of his mouth was foreign. The shape of his lips was different. Somehow, they didn't fit.

Julie quickly entered her apartment and leaned hard against the closed door, her heart thudding, her hands shaking. She didn't turn on the lights, but stood for a long time gazing into the darkness, her mind in turmoil. Paul Shannon had stood between her and Van Hudson that night as if he'd been physically present. The realization made her stomach constrict. Paul. . . .

Oh, dear God, will I never be free of him? she prayed silently into the darkness. But all she could hear in the way of an answer was the electronic hum of a wall clock and the vibrating of her own throbbing pulse.

Paul sat hunched over the too-small dining table—books, papers, and checkbook spread over every square inch.

"What are you doing?" Julie asked cheerfully, letting herself into the apartment.

"Hi, babe," he called. "Paying bills. Very boring." He stretched his long arms over his head and she came up behind him, stood behind his chair, slid her palms down his chest and kissed the top of his curly head. "Now don't distract me," he ordered.

She ignored him and nuzzled his neck. "I'm warning you, I don't need much of an excuse to throw this stuff in the garbage."

"Are we in the red?" she mumbled against his neck, not caring about his answer. His smell was warm, masculine, slightly lime from his aftershave.

"Not quite. By my calculations, we'll have enough left over this month for one movie. No popcorn."

She glanced down at his ledger sheet and the neat tiny rows of numbers. Paul was so organized. Ledger sheets for their pittance of an income. Julie giggled. She scanned the list: rent, electric, grocery, student loan. . . . Something was missing on his sheet. "Where's our tithe?"

"Our what?"

"Our tithe," she said again. "Our 10 percent to God?" Julie had been raised with the idea of tithing. Her parents had done it. She had done it. It was what Scripture required and so she'd always given it gladly.

Paul swiveled his head around and looked at her as if he hadn't heard her correctly. "You must be kidding! We haven't got 10 percent left over."

Her cheeks flamed and suddenly her request did seem ridiculous. "I—I'm sorry. I've just always done it that way."

Paul smiled indulgently and pulled her across his lap tracing his finger along the line of her cheek to the hollow of her throat. "One day, Julie, I'll make plenty of money. Once I graduate in June and pass the bar exam in October, I'm going after the biggest, best firm in this city. Your husband plans to move very quickly up the ladder of success."

His words didn't comfort her. They made her uneasy. Paul had serious plans for his career, and he'd mapped out every step toward accomplishing his goal. He'd deliberately planned to delay taking his bar exams until the fall so that he could avoid the June rush for jobs and be better prepared, once the glut of new lawyers had gotten out of his way. It was a daring and calculated move, but she had no doubt it would work. Paul was a very shrewd man. In the meantime, Julie would keep her jobs and Paul would continue teaching at the law school over the upcoming summer.

"I promise you," he said into her ear, "one day I'll make so much money that you can give 20 percent of it away."

There was something inherently wrong with his logic about giving, but Julie couldn't put it into words. Besides, Paul was leaving a small trail of kisses up her neck and across her throat, and her ability to reason was clouding. "I shouldn't be distracting you," she mumbled halfheartedly.

Julie sighed, deliciously content, as his hands and mouth left a pathway over her warming skin. "No problem," he whispered against her flesh. The vibration of his breath caused her to quiver. "One day I'll dress you in mink."

"I'm allergic to mink," she muttered, reveling in his touch.

"Okay, make it diamonds. How can anyone be allergic to diamonds?"

She caught his face between her hands and stared deeply into his dark eyes. She searched their depths, her heart melting with love, aching with desire for him. "Make it sapphires." Then she buried her face in his hair, breathed in his scent and kissed him with all the love in her soul.

Autumn came to Virginia lovely and golden, dripping in reds and oranges and browns, resplendent in golds and russets and umbers. Autumn—the smell of apples and woodsmoke, the bluster of cold winds, the sound of wood chopping and the crackle of leaves burning. Autumn came and, with it, the poignant memories of long-buried chapters from a book put aside in Julie's mind.

Paul kept his promise. He did not contact her. She only saw him Sundays in church. He came to David Wilson's Bible class, too. She sat on one side of the room, he on the other. She avoided his eyes. Yet she searched the pews for his familiar physique each and every week. And once finding it, she sat far behind him, row upon row behind him, and then let her eyes linger on the back of his dark head.

His black Ferrari attracted the teenage boys of the congregation like flies, and many a Sunday Julie left the parking lot observing Paul's lanky body draped casually against his car, while the boys talked and joked with him. And as October turned into November, she came to expect it. To look for it like some sort of landmark that she could anchor her week to. On Sunday she saw Paul at church. Monday through Friday, she worked. Saturday, she cleaned and shopped and read and occasionally dated Van. And then on Sunday, she saw Paul.

Work continued to mount at the agency as clients pressured for holiday campaigns, commercials, and ads. Julie worked incessantly, and often late. Work was good for her. When she was working, she didn't have time to think. It was the thinking that gnawed at her insides.

"Time out for yogurt?" Tess's face popped around the side of Julie's cubicle at the office. Julie looked up from her typewriter and smiled at her friend's outstretched offering of two cups of yogurt and two plastic spoons.

"Why not?" Julie flipped the switch on her machine. "I could use a break."

"It's after one o'clock," Tess chided. "You could use some lunch." The big-boned woman pulled up a chair and sat down heavily admitting, "I'm whipped."

Julie removed the lid from her yogurt carton and stirred the white substance with the spoon. Soon, streaks of blue ribboned to the top. "Yum, blueberry. You know I like blueberry anything." She eyed Tess and noticed the tired lines at the corners of her eyes and the downward tilt of her mouth. "Bad day, huh?" She wasn't prying, for everyone was overworked this time of the year.

"Bad *night*," Tess corrected.

"Tell me."

"It's Rob," Tess said, grinding her teeth in sudden anger. "He's driving me nuts, Julie. He stays out past curfew. He doesn't study. He's running with some real jerks."

Julie touched Tess's arm. "Honey, I'm so sorry."

"Curse Hank Germaine anyway!" Tess said with heated vehemence. "Why couldn't he have stuck around like a decent father instead of running off to California with that teenage hussy?"

Julie let Tess vent her anger. "Have you talked to Reverend Wilson about Rob?"

"Endlessly," Tess said, letting out a long sigh. "He says to lay down the house rules and enforce them at all costs. He says I can't deviate one iota from my rules. And that infringement must be followed by consistent discipline."

"And?"

Tess smiled ruefully, "So far Rob's grounded until the year 2000."

"Cindy?"

"My joy and my light," Tess sighed. "She's so typically 15. All into hairstyles, clothes, and Jud Ellis." Tess rolled her eyes in feigned exasperation. "And the church youth group. Thank God for that. She loves that youth group and the Freytags. I'll bet they have a hundred things planned for the holidays."

Julie smiled. "If only Rob would get interested in the youth group."

Tess set her half-finished yogurt on Julie's desk and said, "I half think he hates it just to spite me. Just because he knows it's what I want him to do. You want to hear something funny?"

Julie nodded. Tess chose her words carefully. "The one positive male figure Rob seems remotely interested in emulating is Paul Shannon."

Julie absorbed the news and absently stirred the remains of her yogurt. "Paul's very charming," she said staring into the pale purple depths of her carton. "And judging by his comments in Bible class, he does seem to have matured spiritually since I knew him." She set the carton down with great deliberation and smiled brightly at Tess.

Tess responded, but her smile was curious, slightly ironical. " 'Matured spiritually,' " Tess chided. "Is that your way of saying he's changed, after all?"

Julie's cheeks burned and she gave Tess a sheepish smile. "Don't tease me. Maybe he *has* changed. But just like you can't forget what Hank did to you, I can't forget what Paul did to me."

Tess sat quietly for a moment. "I know it seems that I'm sometimes bitter about Hank. But that's just because I get so frustrated about the kids and how he's missing so much of their lives. But, Julie . . ." Tess chose her words with care, "I *did* forgive him."

Her implication made Julie gasp. She looked straight into her friend's face and gawked. "I forgave Paul!" she protested. "I really did!"

Tess gave her a contrite, placating shrug and then quickly changed the subject. "Did you know that Thanksgiving is two weeks away?"

Julie forced herself to focus on Tess's new line of thought. "Yes," her tone was curt.

"How about coming over for the feast to our place? Bring a blueberry pie and I'll do the bird and the trimmings. Cindy would love to see you, and who knows? Maybe Rob will even act human for the occasion."

Julie agreed instantly. She had been dreading the holiday alone. It would be good to be around Tess and her family, regardless of their problems. It would be good to enjoy their company and count her blessings at their table. "Let me bring some apple cider, too," Julie offered. "We can all go to the evening service at the church together. I'll bring a change of clothes."

"You're on!" Tess rose from her chair and headed back to her cubicle, while Julie sat and pondered their conversation for a long time.

"I'm so stuffed, I don't think I can move until Christmas," Julie groaned from the beanbag chair in Tess's rec room.

"Me, too!" Cindy moaned. "Why do people pig out like this every Thanksgiving?" It was a rhetorical question. No one in the room had an answer.

The delicious remains of their Thanksgiving feast lay upstairs like the vestiges of a medieval banquet. The clean-up remained before them, but so far no one had the energy to face it.

"Rob, please turn down the TV," Tess said.

Her voice sounded sharp and Julie winced. The tension was brittle between Rob and his mother.

"Aw, Ma!" Rob complained. "I can't hear the game with all you women blabbing."

Julie looked quickly at the screen, in time to see one football player throw a long pass down the overly green field to an open receiver.

They sat for a few minutes of heavy silence before the phone rang. "I'll get it!" Cindy called, leaping from the sofa and bounding up the stairs. "It's probably Jud."

Rob snorted and Tess stood and stretched. "I'd better start on the kitchen, I can't count on the Good Faeries anymore."

"I'll help," Julie offered, struggling to get out of the

beanbag. But it clung to her overly fed body and she felt like a turtle trying to flip from its back.

"In a minute," Tess said. "Just watch the game for a minute with Rob and let me get mentally prepared for the chore. I'll call you to help. Don't worry."

Julie slung into her beanbag cocoon, watching the football game and stealing covert glances at Rob. The boy's brown hair fell across his forehead stubbornly and his body looked taut and explosive. "You coming to the service with us tonight?" she inquired lightly.

"Guess so," his large shoulders shrugged with rebellious resignation. "If I don't, Mom will flip out."

"But you don't want to go."

Rob turned his troubled hazel eyes on Julie. "All that religion stuff bores me. The place is full of hypocrites." His tone was hostile.

"Rob! That's not true!"

"Everybody spouting about 'family' and 'love'—what a crock!"

Julie felt stunned by the depth of his pent-up vehemence. She knew it was no use arguing with the boy. His mind was made up and a few pious words from her wouldn't change it. "Isn't there anybody there you like?" she asked hopefully.

Rob heaved his shoulders. "Paul Shannon's okay. I can talk to him pretty good. He doesn't talk to me like I'm a kid. Or stupid. Yeah . . . he's okay."

At the mention of Paul's name, Julie tensed. How ironic. How perfectly ironic. Paul had somehow managed to flow over into this aspect of her life, too. She felt like a puppet on strings pulled by . . . ? God? *Unfair. God loves me. And he loves Rob, too,* she reminded herself. But why would He use Paul as an instrument in both their lives? Why was the fabric of her life still colored by Paul's presence? And why was she so afraid of that insight?

"If you don't get out of this kitchen and let me work, I'll never get this Thanksgiving dinner on the table for

our company!" Julie told Paul in complete exasperation. Their tiny kitchen was hardly big enough for her once the oven door was open, much less Paul who had set up residency seemingly under her feet.

"Just checking," he said between mouthfuls of celery.

"Paul!" she cried, setting the partially done turkey on the counter and turning to him. "You're supposed to be stuffing the celery with cream cheese, not stuffing your face with the celery."

He grinned sheepishly. "Did you know you're cute when you're mad? Your eyes get all fiery and your lips pout."

Julie let out an angry snarl and whipped the basting bulb off the counter and began squirting the turkey furiously with its pan juices.

"Besides," Paul said good-humoredly, "it's only Ted and Kathy coming for dinner. And they won't even be here for another hour."

"Well, they have a right to eat on time," she said, piqued at his nonchalance.

"Oh, I get it!" Paul snapped his fingers with sudden understanding. "You've got 'First Holiday' jitters." He leaned against the refrigerator and folded his arms, watching her baste the succulent bird. "I'll bet this is your first turkey!"

"Not true," Julie told him, her back to his angular frame. "Actually it's my second turkey. I married my first one."

For a few moments Paul was completely silent, then he straightened and leaned toward her. "I have been insulted!" His voice filled with mock horror. "By this snip! I, Paul Shannon, soon-to-be attorney at law have been insulted!"

She turned and saw the twinkle in his blue eyes and wicked grin of reprisal on his mouth. She backed into the corner and stabbed the air with her basting bulb in his direction. "Paul, you stay away from me! I mean it!"

He advanced and in one quick motion seized her around the waist and lifted her up off the floor. "Paul!"

she shrieked. "Let me go! I'm warning you . . . !" She dropped the bulb and writhed in his iron grip.

He carried her kicking and threatening into the living room. She twisted sharply and momentarily slipped from his grasp. But her victory was short-lived as Paul recaptured her and brought her with him into a heap on the floor. They wrestled wildly for a few moments, Julie shoving and flailing to escape his strong hands and powerful arms.

"Let go of me!" she cried, laughter welling up in her throat. "I mean it, Paul. Let go of me or you'll never eat turkey dinner!"

"Ladies and gentlemen of the jury!" Paul began once he had pinned her arms over her head and thrown his leg over her struggling body. He raised his head and addressed the surrounding furniture. "I have in my custody a wisp of a woman who has called me—her lord and master—a 'turkey!' Surely, this act of unprovoked aggression cannot go unpunished!"

Julie lurched suddenly and almost succeeded in throwing him off. But his denim-clad thigh pushed hard against her hips and pinned her helplessly beneath him again. "I ask you!" Paul continued into the room, "What is a fitting punishment for this misdemeanor?"

"No fair!" Julie yelled. "I have no representation! I wasn't even read my rights!"

He studied her, his face inches from her own. Her breath came in gasps and she saw his face, flushed, his eyes glowing and brilliant in the afternoon light. A surge shot through her that bordered on physical hunger. She heaved against his chest in futile struggle.

"Irrelevant!" he said, his breath warm on her skin. "The verdict is 'guilty.' The punishment," he paused, watching her mouth for a few tension ladened moments, ". . . torture by tickling!" He fell on her then, and they rolled about on the floor, Julie squealing and twisting from his fingers and hands that poked and prodded and tickled.

"Stop-that-Paul! You-know-I-can't-stand-that!" she

wailed between hiccups of uncontrollable giggles. "I'm-warning-you! I'll-get-even!" But he continued, undaunted by her protests and her threats of retaliation. Minutes later, they collapsed together in an exhausted heap, Julie gasping and gulping air, Paul still encircling her with his arms.

"Had enough?" he asked impishly.

"Neanderthal!" she accused. His head jerked up. "No! No!" she cried, seeing his intent for renewed attack across his features.

"Do you know what your problem is, Mrs. Shannon?"

"You!" she retorted. "You're cutting off my circulation and causing me to make dinner run late."

He ignored her. "Your problem is your mouth. It's always getting you into trouble."

She heard his voice grow tender and a tingle shot up her spine. His desire for her flamed in his slant-set eyes giving him the look of a pacing, stalking cat, and his mouth moved to within inches of hers. She stared into his eyes, losing herself in the pools of cobalt blue. "Our company will be here in less than an hour," she mumbled, not really caring. "And dinner's going to be late," she warned, already slipping her arms around his neck.

"To quote a famous queen," Paul whispered huskily, " 'Let them eat cake.' " And his mouth descended to hers, lifting her up in wave after wave of pulsating emotion. . . .

They did eat—three hours later. "Good grief, Julie," Ted grumbled once they had all been seated around the small table top, set with her best for Thanksgiving dinner. "My stomach thinks my throat's been cut. If I'd known dinner was going to be this late, Kathy and I would have slept in longer."

Kathy shot him a withering glance and Julie smiled sweetly. Paul stood, carving the juicy brown crusted turkey. "Julie was preoccupied," Paul offered.

"Busy?" Ted asked, not understanding the look that passed between his hosts.

"Yeah," Paul added blandly, "jury duty."

The church service was late getting started. The organist played longer than usual and the congregation began to shift in the pews, expectantly. David Wilson was late starting the Thanksgiving Eve service. Uncharacteristically late.

Beside Julie, Rob, too, shifted and fidgeted, glancing around the pews in unconcealed annoyance. "Wonder what's going on?" Cindy whispered to her mother seated on the other side of Rob. Julie searched the front of the church, but Reverend Wilson was not in his usual chair next to the pulpit. The assistant pastor glanced at his watch and made a motion to the organist to play another interlude.

As usual, the church was packed. A further testimony to the power and charisma of the vibrant young minister, Julie thought. Paul was there. Julie had seen him when she'd arrived with Tess's family. She'd felt his eyes on them as they'd settled in the pews, but she'd not glanced back at him. Paul had waved. But Julie stubbornly refused to acknowledge his presence—or his effect on her.

Grudgingly, she realized he'd not missed one church service. He'd attended every Sunday, been visible in every Bible study class, every group session that David taught. There had been a time when his devotion to the Word would have thrilled her. Now, it only made her suspicious. What was he attempting to gain? In the past, Paul hadn't done anything that didn't benefit him in some way.

Her attention was diverted when the side door next to the high-mounted pulpit opened and David stepped out, adjusting his robes as he entered. An almost audible sigh went up from the parishioners with his arrival. But something was wrong. Julie could see it in the tenseness of his body, in the troubled look on his usually peaceful features.

David motioned for the organist to stop and then climbed into the pulpit. The congregation grew hushed and expectant. An ominous feeling stole over Julie, causing her heart to beat faster. Reverend Wilson had news for them all. And somehow, Julie sensed it was not good news.

David cleared his throat and said, "Forgive my late entrance. But I've been at the hospital all afternoon."

A ripple of whispers flowed through the crowd. He continued, "This afternoon Mary Freytag went into premature labor. The doctors tried to stop her contractions with drugs. But they couldn't. At five o'clock today she delivered a 2 pound 5 ounce premature boy. He's alive. But *only* by the grace of God."

CHAPTER 5

AN AUDIBLE GASP SWEPT the congregation and Cindy released a small cry. Instinctively, Julie reached over Rob to touch her, seeing tears spring into the girl's eyes. She felt the sharp stab of tears prick at her own eyes.

"Let me repeat," David said with authority from the pulpit, "the baby is alive. For that we are all most grateful to God. And Mary's doing fine. There were no complications with the delivery. However, these next few days will be critical." David paused while the impact of his message seeped through the benumbed people.

Julie released her clenched fist in her lap, willing herself to concentrate on David's words. *Poor Mary! Poor Don. Poor baby!* her thoughts whirled over and over. *Two pounds! Why that's no heavier than a good-sized book.*

"After the service tonight," David said, his calm and soothing voice bringing a semblance and order to Julie's ragged thoughts, "I want to hold a prayer vigil for the baby. Many of you are gifted prayer intercessors. Please come up after the service and let's pray together. God

66

is merciful. God is just. Let us beseech Him together on behalf of this fragile life."

Julie determined to join with the prayer warriors after the service. If it was all she could do for the Freytags, then she'd do it with all her heart.

"I have another request," David continued. "It's something for all of you to think about and pray about. As you know, the Freytags are our youth leaders." Cindy sniffed and stiffled a shuddering sob. Julie patted her shoulder while Tess held the teen's hand. "We're going to need someone to volunteer to take their place . . . at least through the next several months.

"Please pray about it," David directed. "Our kids in the kingdom of God need responsible, godly supervision and direction. If God speaks to you about helping them out, please contact me privately over the next few days." David paused. "Now," he said, "it's Thanksgiving. God has loved us enough to shower us with His bounteous blessings. Let's begin to thank Him with hymn 604."

The next few days dragged by for Julie with agonizing slowness. She had the entire Thanksgiving weekend off and she used the time to pray for the Freytag infant and to console and comfort Cindy. They called and checked daily on the infant's welfare. The report was always the same: Critical.

He had immature lungs; a respirator did his breathing. He had an immature digestive tract; a tube in his throat fed him. And his heartbeat was erratic and unstable. But after three days, he was still alive.

Something else nagged at Julie. She couldn't forget David's plea for youth group counselors. She felt it was something she should volunteer to do. She had little experience. But she had a great love for Cindy and even sullen Rob. She knew that the youth group should have the opportunity to complete their plans for the holiday season, and she felt that she needed to be more useful to the church.

In the almost five years that she'd attended the church, Julie had given little back to this congregation of fellow believers. She owed them. She owed God. She set up an appointment with David Wilson in his church office for the following Monday night and determined to offer herself for this service. Reverend Wilson would determine if she could do it. She trusted him to discern God's will for her in the matter.

"Hello, Julie!" David rose from his study desk and greeted her with a warm handshake. His generous smile and enthusiasm melted all her reservations about asking him for the opportunity to serve the church and its youth. "Sit down," he invited, and settled her into a leather desk chair across from his own behind the desk.

His study lookes like him, Julie thought with a surreptitious glance at the room. It was tan and camel colored, very masculine, with three walls laden with bookshelves. His desk top was a maze of intimate clutter, a stack of papers, a pile of pink phone message slips, an open Bible, and two wooden-framed photographs of his family. One of Sharon looking beguiling and a little sexy. And one of Sharon holding their two sons, looking like a proper young mother. Julie realized that David and his wife must share a special relationship, and the knowledge sent a pang of unexpected melancholy through her.

David leaned back and appraised Julie with his light brown eyes. "What can I do for you?"

"Well . . . I was hoping that I might do something for you. And this church," she added hastily. "Reverend, I'd like to volunteer for that job as youth counselor."

A light flickered in his eyes. "Call me David," he said, then pressed his fingertips together, weighing her request.

"I don't have any real experience," she said defensively, "but I know I could do it with a little guidance and direction."

"That's very interesting," David mused. "But the

68

job calls for a couple. The girls need a woman to relate to; the boys, a man."

In spite of herself, Julie felt her disappointment keenly. "Well," she shrugged. "I—I just felt that it was something I should offer. Thanks, anyway."

"Don't be so hasty," David said, preventing her from rising. "As it turns out I've had a single man volunteer, too. If you'd be willing to work with him, maybe you both could lead the group and fulfill what God has obviously asked both of you to do."

Julie listened, intrigued. "Perhaps you know him?" David continued. "He's new, but has excellent credentials. Paul Shannon. . . ." At the mention of Paul's name, the color drained from Julie's face.

Seeing her reaction, David tipped his head and a puzzled frown knit his brow. "Is something wrong, Julie? I've talked with Mr. Shannon at length. He's taught with the YMCA in the city where he used to live. And he's been a Big Brother there, too." The news surprised Julie almost as much as the mention of his name. "He's really very qualified," David finished.

"I—it's not that . . ." Julie stammered, feeling flushed and agitated. "It's . . . it's just that. . . ." She couldn't find the words she wanted, realizing with a jolt that no one in Washington, except Tess, knew anything about her past. Not even her minister. Julie took a deep breath and committed herself to tell David the truth. She'd hid it long enough and now it had come back to haunt her.

"Rev . . . David," she corrected. "I . . . there's something you don't know about me."

He didn't speak, but his warm eyes encouraged her to plunge ahead. "I'm divorced."

His face never changed. "Unfortunately, many Christians are."

"There's more. When I moved to Washington five years ago, I was very newly divorced. And very, very hurt," she confessed, tense, chagrined to feel how much it still hurt to rake over the past. "I took back my maiden name, Kreel. My married name was Shannon. Paul Shannon is my ex-husband."

Once the truth was out, she released her breath all at once, raising her eyes to David's for comfort and acceptance. She found both. "I see . . ." David mused, giving meaning to his words she did not fathom.

"I don't really understand why he moved to Washington all of a sudden. He said it was a job offer," she continued, anxious to have all of the story out. "It's been harder to see him again than I ever imagined it would. But under the circumstances, it would be very difficult for me to work with him. I'm sorry. Since he's more qualified than me, I'll bow out." The last words came in a rush and left her breathless.

David raised his hand, palm out, a gesture to stop her words of dismissal. "Don't be so hasty, Julie. I understand some things now. Thank you for confiding in me." He watched her for a moment. She wanted to leave, but didn't feel he was finished talking to her. David started again, choosing words that intrigued her. "Would it surprise you to know that Sharon has had a prayer burden for you these last two months?"

It did. David continued, "You've been on her heart for a long time. I think I understand why now. Please, don't bow out yet, Julie. Pray about it. *Really* pray about it. Ask God to reveal His will to you about working with Paul. And it wouldn't hurt to sit down and discuss it with Paul, either." He finished with a gentle smile. "Don't let your confused feelings sit around in the dark. Confront them. Throw a little light on them. Jesus said that light is always preferable to darkness."

Julie offered acceptance that she didn't feel. "Fair enough," she said, more skeptical than she intended.

"Good!" David beamed her a smile. "Then come back in a few days and let me know what God has told you." He rose and escorted her to the door.

"Thank you, David."

He gave her a beguiling half-smile. "I'm your pastor, Julie. Any time you want to talk, let me know." She knew he was opening the door for her to confide her divorce trauma to him. She never had talked it out. Not with a minister, anyway. That thought disturbed her. Why hadn't she ever done that? Why had she guarded it and her feelings so carefully all this time? She had no answers.

Julie pulled on her trenchcoat and stepped out into the dark drizzle of the November night.

"Oh, Paul, that robe makes you look so distinguished!" Julie bubbled as Paul adjusted the scarlet cowl over his graduation gown. They stood in their bedroom, in front of the vanity mirror, surveying his black-clad image.

He gave her a lopsided grin and tapped the tip of her ... "We made it, baby! This time tomorrow, I'll be an official graduate of law school. And once I pass the bars in October . . . I'll be ready to take on the world."

Her heart swelled and she slid happily into his arms, feeling the soft material of the robe against her cheek. He smoothed her hair. "Maybe I'll be a judge someday," he mused.

She stepped back and eyed him from head to toe. "Actually, you look more like a 'fallen' choirboy," she teased.

"Nasty remark. This time next year, Julie, I'll be set with a firm and we'll be raking in the money."

"Good! I'm dying to quit work."

"You don't mean that?" Paul asked, his voice taking on a serious tone.

"Of course I do!" Julie confirmed, wary at his unexpected response. "I'm tired of working, Paul. I want to stay at home, do housewifey things and get pregnant." She shot him a flirtatious smile which he did not return. Julie sobered. "You do want to have babies, don't you?"

Paul shrugged. "Oh, sure, someday . . ." he gestured vaguely into the air. "But we've got so much to do first. I need to establish myself in my profession. I'd like us to buy a house, a car, maybe join a country club. . . ."

Julie felt her mouth drop open. "Paul! You're not serious? A country club?" Her tone was incredulous. "How plebeian! How upwardly mobile." Her eyes grew wide with disbelief.

Paul shot her a grin. "Country clubs are part of career planning, Julie. A necessary evil. Don't be a snob."

"And babies aren't part of the 'career plan?' " she asked, her tone more hurt than inquisitive.

"Not now," Paul said with finality. "Aw, look, honey," he said pulling her into the dark folds of his robe, "we'll have plenty of time for babies. A whole lifetime. But not now." He raised his hands to her shoulders and pushed her away until he was looking down at her, full in the face. His blue eyes were serious, his fingers firm and purposeful. "And Julie, I don't want any 'surprises,' " he stressed evenly, his words sounding more like a warning than a request. "We'll plan babies together. Do you understand? No surprises."

She nodded her acquiescence, feeling drained and somewhat hollow inside. She longed to have his baby. And now he'd said "No." Her arms felt heavy and strangely empty.

Julie did pray about it. She sought God daily for an answer. Asked Him nightly to reveal His will to her. But at the end of the week she was no closer to knowing about the youth counselor position than she'd been on Monday. By Friday, she was more confused than ever, dreading Sunday and facing David again with no answer.

On Saturday, she decided to go to the hospital and see the Freytag baby, hoping that it would put her problem into a better perspective. But she dreaded that, too. She wasn't sure she could stand to see that tiny infant, struggling so valiantly for his life.

The nursery in the hospital was painted a gay yellow, and large cartoon cut-outs adorned the walls. Smurfs, Big Bird, the Peanuts gang looked down from the walls on the rows of lucite carts that held a pride of newborn infants. Julie stood at the nursery window watching the tiny, bundled babies as nurses walked between carts, holding one, tucking in another, changing a third.

Babies. So many babies. Some with heads of dark, silky hair. Some blond and pink-faced. Some bald and wrinkled. Her eyes swept over them. Some slept peacefully, eyelashes fringing the slits of their closed eyes. Others screamed, their fists clutched tightly on both sides of their heads. Silent wails, prevented from penetrating into the viewing room by the thick pane of safety glass. Julie watched, her eyes lingering on each one, pressed on each side by relatives and siblings, straining to see "their" baby.

"Look, Joel. There's your brother. Oh, honey, he looks just like your dad."

"I tell you, Theresa, he's the biggest kid in there. Look at that. Ten pounds! What a whopper!"

Julie felt a smile curve her lips. She read the name tags on each lucite cart. "Male, Moffat." "Female, Elam." She did not know these people. But she shared their joy. With a sigh, Julie stepped away from that particular nursery window to the next one. This room was different.

It still held carts of babies, but there were fewer in here. This room housed the premies, the sick ones, the struggling ones. Her eyes found him at once. "Male, Freytag." *How little he is!* Something clutched in Julie's throat as she gazed at the tiny scrap of human life that lay in the protective bubble of an incubator.

He was so small! Hooked to a maze of tubes and wires and machines! A glob of white tape crisscrossed his mouth and nose, holding the breathing and feeding tubes in place. She watched the rapid rise and fall of his papery thin chest and followed the lead wires strapped to it to the blipping box that showed his heartbeat. The green blip flickered steadily across the screen over and over, time after time. Her vision began to blur.

"He's a fighter, you know." Paul's voice startled her

73

and surprised her so much that at first it didn't register that he was standing next to her at the nursery window. When it did register, she was at a loss for words.

He wore his cashmere overcoat. But underneath he was dressed more casually in a burgundy crewneck sweater and denim jeans, faded and worn from years of use. Finally, she managed to ask, "How . . . how long have you been standing there?"

"Long enough. Come on," he urged firmly, reaching out and taking her elbow. "Let me buy you a cup of coffee."

She wanted to protest, but she couldn't. Deep down she was grateful. Grateful to have someone help her to make the simple decision to leave.

He took her down to the hospital coffee shop. It was crowded, filled with visitors, personnel, doctors, nurses. But he found them a corner table, pulled out her chair, removed his coat, and settled across from her, his long legs folded and tucked into the too-small space. He pushed his sweater up to his elbows, exposing his corded lower arms and their dark curling hair. Julie was acutely aware of her intimate knowledge of his habits and gestures.

"Two coffees," he told the harried waitress and after the woman poured them, he slid her the stainless cream pitcher and two packets of Sweet 'n Low, reflexively, because he knew her habits, too.

"David tells me you volunteered to work with the youth group," Paul began, taking her mind off the baby upstairs and focusing it back on her dilemma.

She smiled inwardly, wryly. Paul, the counselor, the lawyer, always asking the right questions, always probing for the unexpressed words, shifting and shuffling her thoughts and emotions. "Yes, I'm not sure what to do." *At least that's honest,* she told herself.

His probing blue eyes looked at her, serious from their slanted set in his face. Dark, clipped curls, once errant, now styled and groomed, trailed onto his forehead. Her hand itched to touch them. But she did not.

74

"Julie, we can work on this together if you'll let us. I want to work with those kids. I want to work with you. But I don't want me to be the one to keep you from taking the job."

His plea was so simple, so eloquent, she had to drop her eyes to her coffee cup in order to keep her wits about her. "How do you know so much about kids? And working with them?" She hedged his indirect question.

"After . . ." he searched for words, struggling to avoid the topic they both knew she couldn't discuss. "After we broke up and you moved away, I left the Rinaldi firm." Something fluttered in her stomach. He hurried on. "I took a long hard look at my life. I was alone . . . absolutely alone. For the first time in my life, Paul Shannon couldn't solve his own problems.

"I immediately joined another firm." A grin tugged at the corner of his mouth. "I figured that if I worked hard enough, I'd be in control of my life again. But, fortunately, God had other plans for me." He stirred his coffee absently, letting his confession settle into her spirit before continuing his narrative.

"I volunteered to work in a community storefront law practice, helping people who couldn't afford legal aid. I got involved with a local YMCA, working with kids. Most were from broken homes. Abused. Down and out." He shrugged. "It was a challenge and I liked it."

"Two of my coworkers had a street ministry and led some of the local kids to the Lord. And I mean tough kids. Street punks. I'd seen the streets from both sides, and frankly the ministry's results were a lot longer-lasting than mine—on the legal side.

"Through one of those men, I started attending a home Bible study group. We met once a week, reading, studying, praying. The Bible came alive for me. I saw myself in a whole new light. And I didn't like what I saw. I did a lot of repenting," his voice almost broke.

"That little study-prayer group changed my life," his

voice took on a low, passionate quality. "It's important to me that you know that, Julie. It was hard for me to see my true nature . . ." his words trailed. "But once I was saved, a life in Christ became my highest goal. I identified with Saul in the Book of Acts."

She let her eyes rest comfortably on his face as he spoke, attracted by the passion of his revelation.

"I think I understood how he felt after his encounter with Christ on the road to Damascus. Here he was, once powerful and rich and arrogant," a tiny smile curved the right corner of Paul's mouth, "reduced to hiding in a room, blind, helpless, dependent on some strange man to teach him, disciple him, train him. But I'm convinced that that's where God really met Saul. There in that darkness. In his weakness."

A lump rose in Julie's throat. She swallowed against it. "I—I know that Rob thinks a lot of you, Paul," she redirected the conversation, keeping her voice steady. She accepted his words, but was hesitant to plunge ahead emotionally too quickly.

Paul laughed and his eyes twinkled. "Rob likes my car," he joked. He added, "He's a good kid, Julie. Mixed up, bitter about his runaway father, but I've seen a lot harder nuts to crack. Believe me, Rob Germaine belongs to the Lord."

His confidence spilled over to Julie and it buoyed her spirits. She knew suddenly that she was going to become responsible for the youth group with him. She knew she would take the job. She wanted to tell Paul how she felt, but she wanted to put conditions and limits on their personal relationship.

"I have a personal affinity for Rob's sister, Cindy," Julie confessed.

"You mean the girl who always speaks in superlatives and moons over Jud all the time?"

Julie laughed aloud, "That's the one!" She was amazed at how simple it was to talk to him. And surprised at how much she had missed it. It was almost like when they'd first met . . . but different. There was a gentleness in him and a depth that beckoned and called to her. *Watch it!* her mind warned. *Don't get sucked in.* Julie struggled against the old memories that threatened to surface. *Forward. I have to move forward. The past is dead.*

"I—I think we can be a team with the youth group," Julie said soberly, emphasizing the words "youth group." The group was safe. It was a common ground where they could meet, uncluttered by the network of the past. It was a fresh start.

Paul smiled, the slow, lazy smile she'd always loved. The one that began in his sapphire eyes and worked its way down to his sensuous, full mouth and filled her with such a warm, dewy feeling inside. "I understand," he told her. "And I agree. We'll make a good team with the kids."

The September afternoon was hot and muggy. The law school get-acquainted mixer was crowded into the ground floor of Nathan Hall, and the clusters of eager, newly accepted students, returning students, professors, student aides and their assorted wives, husbands, and lovers were crammed into the too-small room on the too-hot day.

The old wooden floors of the lecture hall groaned under the shifting weight of the milling people and pale sunlight filtered in through the open windows, inviting a nonexistent breeze to enter. Nathan Hall was an architectural landmark to the university, dating back to the 1800s. "They should have condemned it fifty years ago," Julie thought angrily, seeing no beauty in the aged oak and poorly insulated walls.

She and Paul had been there two hours already and Julie had a mind-splitting headache. Her temples throbbed and pounded and her stomach felt queasy from the incessant aching. The noise droned around her like a persistent insect until the very walls appeared to be closing in on her. She hadn't wanted to come in the first place. After working all week at the agency and all day

Saturday at the law library, she was exhausted and physically drained.

But Paul had wanted to come. Her mouth twisted at the memory of their argument over it. They'd fought heatedly about it, each demanding that the other be more considerate of the other's needs, feelings, wants. "It's important," Paul had shouted. "I can't sit for the bars until next month. I have to keep this job as a student assistant. It'll put me in touch with the incoming students. Plus keep me in touch with the university."

"You've been 'in touch' with the university all summer," she'd countered heatedly. "We've both worked day and night. We never have any time together. We're always looking out for your career! I'm tired, Paul. I want to stay home!"

He'd won, of course. Paul always won. Maybe because she was just too tired to fight. Julie sucked in her breath and cruised the room with her eyes. Such bright eager faces! Students struggling to set their feet on the paths of glory! Her mouth twisted ironically.

Paul stood off to the side, in heated debate with the law school dean and Ted. He and Kathy had another year. Thank God it's over for us, Julie thought grimly. She watched Paul debate, leaning forward, intense, commanding. He always reminded her of a runner, poised, waiting for the starting gun.

He was good. He'd get his perfect job. She was sure of that. But at what cost? Funny, she thought meanly, he has the energy for this stuff, but he can't even spend an hour in church with me. That topic had caused another argument earlier that same morning. She'd lost that one, too. Two strikes, Julie, she told herself ruefully.

"You look like you're being tortured," Kathy said in her ear.

Julie gave a start and turned to the short-haired blond. She forced a smile. "I have a rotten headache."

"Yeah, I'd get one, too, if I thought Ted would leave right now. Why do the powers-that-be insist on holding this shindig in this miserable place each year instead of *one of those nice, new air-conditioned halls on the campus?" Kathy griped.*

"Tradition," Julie offered. "We certainly wouldn't want to change 'tradition' for the sake of comfort and convenience."

Their complaints were interrupted by Paul and Ted, still hashing over their discussion. Paul slipped his arm around Julie's waist and kissed her absently on the cheek. She gritted her teeth. For some reason, the gesture infuriated her.

"Hey, Shannon," Ted said suddenly, conspiratorily. "Take a look over there by the door. Look who just came in."

Heads turned. Julie saw her at once. And so did every red-blooded man in the room. The woman who stood, gracing the room with her presence, was so beautiful that she took Julie's breath away. She was tall, willowy, and tawny gold. Her hair, her eyes, her skin, all gleamed with a golden aura that reminded Julie of a lioness. Not just her coloring. But the look in her eyes as well. She had the look of a huntress—earthy, challenging. And the smell of money all but clung to her shapely body. Her dress was the hue of carmeled silk. Her shoes, Gucci leather. Gold chains, subtle, tasteful, shimmered from her throat and her wrist. Her hands were ringless.

"My heart, be still," Ted mumbled under his breath, uttering what every person in the room was thinking.

"Eyes front, lover-boy," Kathy snapped at his side. "Or I'll scratch them out."

"Aw, baby," Ted said, focusing his attention on Kathy's threatening face. "You know I'm just like a dog who chases cars. What would I do if I caught one?"

Paul laughed aloud. "Who is she?" Julie watched his eyes. She watched as they appraised the woman, sweeping and analyzing her beauty.

Jealousy pricked at her. Hot pricks of gnawing, chewing jealousy. By comparison, Julie felt colorless and dowdy. Her pale yellow shirtwaist seemed girlish and outdated. She hated herself for not taking more care to

79

*dress for the mixer. Her hairstyle felt old-fashioned, too,
her hair shapeless and tangled, limp with the heat. She
should have gotten it cut.*

*The woman moved graciously through the room, to
cluster after cluster of people. Obviously, she felt perfectly at home with the professors, the dean, the
administration.*

"She's Bianca Rinaldi," *Ted answered as if he'd just
introduced some famous diplomat.*

"You mean the Bianca Rinaldi?" *Paul asked, his eyes
scanning the woman with renewed appreciation.*

"So what?" *Kathy snapped. Julie was eaten with curiosity, too. She felt left out, like she'd missed the punch-
line of a joke.*

"Rinaldi, Fuller and Wellington is the biggest, oldest
law firm in this city," *Paul explained, his eyes never
leaving the woman's journey around the room.* "Bianca
is Robert Rinaldi's daughter. A junior partner, too, I
understand. I'd heard she was teaching a course in Corporate Ethics this semester. I just had no idea that's
what she looked like."

"Nepotism," *Julie muttered hatefully, taking a dislike
to the graceful creature, whose laugh sounded as golden
as the rest of her.*

*Paul arched an eyebrow at Julie, letting his arm loosen
and drop from around her waist.* "That's unfair, Julie.
She had to earn her credentials just like the rest of us.
She had to pass the bars like any other graduate. And
she'd have to be pretty bright to be offered a teaching
position here at the university."

*Bianca arrived at their group on the arm of the dean.
Julie wished she could fade into the walls, feeling common and unattractive next to the tawny-haired beauty.
Introductions were made and Julie noticed that Bianca
didn't talk—she purred. Her voice was low and throaty,
mellow and soft. She dragged her vowels together when
she spoke, adding further to her feline image.*

"Dean Stanford's spoken most highly of you, Mr.
Shannon," *Bianca purred, her voice thick, like golden*

80

honey. "I understand you'll be working with one of the classes I'll be teaching. I'm looking forward to working with you."

Julie watched as Paul nodded, his eyes narrowed, appraising. She saw his senses stir, keenly aware of the woman's feminine mystique. Julie wanted to reach out and clutch his arm. She wanted to shout, "This one is mine." But she did not. Because she was, after all, civilized. And civilized people didn't do things like that. So she stood and watched, helplessly, feeling the electricity snap and hum in the air between Bianca and Paul.

It wasn't until much later that Julie realized Paul had never even introduced her as his wife.

CHAPTER 6

"YOU'RE GOING TO TAKE OVER the youth group with Mr. Shannon, Julie? Really! Oh, it's just too much! I can't stand it!" Cindy cried in her animated style, throwing her arms around Julie's neck, impulsively. "I've got to go call Tina. How positively *fabulous*. I'm gonna call Jud, too!" The bubbling, bouncing teen fairly whirled out of the living room, leaving an amused Julie and her amazed mother together in her wake.

"Is the hurricane gone?" Julie asked, flopping on Tess's sofa with a grin.

Tess nodded, but her face did not lose its disbelieving expression. "You've agreed to work with Paul with the kids?"

Julie blushed slightly, squirming under Tess's penetrating gaze. "Just with the kids," she stated. "David needed the help and Paul and I agreed we could work out our differences long enough to supervise the kids. He's good for Rob. You said that yourself," Julie reminded Tess.

Her friend curled her feet under herself on the red sofa and nodded in agreement. "Yes, he is. I have no reservations about the two of you helping the youth group. But will you be able to keep your personal lives apart?"

Julie toyed with a fluffy sofa cushion, saying, "Positively. David knows about our divorce. And he knows how I feel about Paul. The kids need never know. And just as soon as the Freytags are able to pick up the reins again, I'm finished. So get that twinkle out of your eyes, old friend," Julie bristled at the look crossing Tess's face. "This is just a temporary arrangement. Paul and I are coworkers in the church for a few months. And that's *all*!"

Tess batted innocent eyelashes at Julie from behind her lavender-tinted glasses. "Entire kingdoms have been subdued in less time," Tess drawled pointedly. Suddenly, she sobered. "Word of advice from an old friend? Take off your blinders. Look at Paul with your spiritual eyes and not through your hurt. You'll be surprised at what you see."

Julie blushed hotly, indignant at Tess's implication. "We're divorced. Paul and I made our choices a long time ago. There's nothing left for us, Tess. Nothing!"

Julie arrived at the Freytag house at a little after seven. Paul's Ferrari was already parked in the driveway. He'd arranged the meeting, called her at her office and advised her of it. She still remembered how her heart had hammered at the sound of his voice on her telephone.

"Don wants us to come over and get their files and project information as soon as possible," Paul explained. "Mary's home and doing fine, but she goes to the hospital twice a day to be with the baby, and Don wants the youth group off her mind."

"Sure," Julie said, clutching the receiver. How could the sound of his voice rattle her so? "I'll meet you there tonight after work."

Don opened the door and brought her into the family room where Mary sat in an overstuffed chair and Paul stood gazing into a red-brick fireplace. As Paul's eyes

83

swept over her, she tried not to be affected by them. He'd obviously come straight from his office as he still wore an immaculately cut brown suit, a pale peach-colored shirt with a contrasting white collar and a brown silk tie. It was loosened at his throat.

"Mary," Julie walked quickly to the pale-faced woman in the chair and hugged her warmly. "How are you? And the baby?"

"Joshua," Mary told her. "We named him Joshua. It means 'the Lord saves.' " She smiled wanly. "He's holding on."

Don cleared his throat and said, "We really appreciate the way you and Paul have stepped in to help us. I have all the material here in these cardboard boxes. Let's start."

The four of them sat in the cozy room for two hours, scanning the material and discussing the upcoming agenda. There was so much to do! Caroling parties. Christmas decorations for the sanctuary. A special Christmas party at a nearby home for the elderly. A Christmas party and gift exchange for the kids themselves. The list seemed endless! Julie's head swam with all the details.

"Then, of course, there's the annual camping retreat the second week of June," Don said, shifting through another stack of papers.

"Camping retreat?" Julie asked.

"Oh, you know, Julie," Don said. "We do it every year. But just with the high schoolers. There's only nine of them—five girls and four boys."

Julie gave Paul an apprehensive look. He raised an eyebrow and let an amused smile play across his mouth. "Julie's idea of roughing it is a Holiday Inn without a pool."

Julie shot him a scathing glance. She didn't want the Freytags to know anything about their former mutual past. And the comment had been far too intimate for her tastes. But Don let the remark slide, as if he hadn't heard it.

"Oh, you'll love it!" Don assured Julie. "I mean it. Mary and I always get more out of it than the kids. Don't we, hon?"

Mary smiled, enforcing his testimony. "It's the truth. We pitch tents, cook over open campfires, hike, do Bible study, and meditate on the Word. It's a wonderful week and you always come back refreshed and spiritually renewed."

"We've already picked out the trail," Don added, spreading open a Virginia State map for Paul and Julie. "See." He pointed to a red circled area. "Up here in the Blue Ridges, near the National Park. It's beautiful country. The perfect place to spend a week. We also planned a canoe trip down this river." His finger followed a curved blue line down the map.

Julie swallowed and smiled gamely. "Maybe you'll be able to take over before then," she suggested, half-hoping they'd agree.

"Oh, I don't think so," Don said.

"Probably not," Mary confirmed. "Once Joshua weighs five pounds and we get to bring him home, I'm going to want to stay with him until I'm sure he's strong and healthy."

Dismay crossed Julie's thoughts. *Why this job's going to last over six months!* She hadn't considered that sort of time frame. Six months of working side by side with Paul. What had she gotten herself into?

His eyes locked with hers and a faint grin tugged at the corners of his mouth. She shot him daggers. Six months. Or six years. It didn't matter. She was never going to let herself become involved with Paul Shannon again. Like the sting of a scorpion, the hurt was something she'd never forget.

"I thought you'd be happy about it, Julie!" Paul said hotly across their bedroom. I thought you'd be glad for me. Instead, you're acting like a shrew about a great job opportunity." He yanked off his shirt, exposing the lean, muscled chest.

Julie felt her own anger rise to meet his. "Happy! Why should I be happy because you're a law clerk with the Rinaldi firm?" She tugged her brush through her hair with such fury that a hunk of hair came out in it. "Besides," she retorted, "you haven't sat for your exams yet. How can they hire you?"

"Contingency. Firms do it all the time. They hire whom they want, then take care of the paperwork. Don't you see, baby," he stressed, crossing the room in several long strides. He placed his hands on her shoulders and caught her eyes in the vanity mirror. "This is my big break. The Rinaldi firm gets hundreds of applications from aspiring lawyers. And I'm in on the ground floor. What a place to begin my career!"

The intensity of his explanation only made her angrier. "Your career!" She fairly spat out the words. "That's all you ever think about."

His blue eyes grew cold and steely. "What I do, I do for us," he said, the muscles in his jaw clenching.

She held his eyes for a moment, then purposefully shrugged off his hands. "Not for me, Paul, I don't care one bit about how much money you make."

His mouth twisted into a bitter line. "You will some-day, baby. Someday when you want a nice house, fancy clothes, kids in private schools."

Something in his face warned her not to push him on the topic. Julie resumed brushing her long black hair, more slowly, deliberately. "And just how are you going to get downtown to the office everyday?"

"The bus, like you. Or maybe Ms. Rinaldi will give me a lift."

The look on her face stopped him cold. "How convenient." Her tone was deadly calm, filled with innuendo.

He met her eyes in the mirror again and his words came with such deadly control, that she was momentarily frightened. "Green is a very ugly color on you, Julie. And jealousy is a very un-Christian emotion."

She leaped to her feet and whirled around, so angry

she could only sputter. "How dare you question my values! How dare you judge me!"

Paul rocked back on his heels and jammed his hands into his pockets. "I'm going out," he said tersely, dismissing her like she was a truculent child.

"Good!" she shot heatedly. "I needed to catch up on my reading anyway!" She aimed her words like arrows, pointing them directly at the area of their life where they'd always found satisfaction and completion. She said it to hurt him—to make him pay for his attitude and his dismissal of her feelings.

He stared at her, his face a stony mask. For a minute she wasn't sure what he was going to do and she recoiled at the prospects of his fury. But he calmly turned, picked up his shirt off the chair where he'd laid it and said, "Don't wait up."

When the door closed behind him, she hurled the brush against it. It splintered the wood and chipped the paint. But it did not bring him back.

"Don't tell me you're having second thoughts already!" The question came from David Wilson. Julie sat in his office, twisting her hands nervously in her lap.

She felt like a traitor and a coward, but she couldn't help herself. She'd never dreamed she'd have to spend so much time with Paul over plans for the youth group. "I—it's just awkward!" Julie told the minister. "We don't even have neutral territory to meet in."

"Use the church," David offered. "That's what it's here for. We have plenty of rooms available and plenty of people knocking around every night for meetings, discussions, Bible study. The list is endless."

That solution hadn't occurred to her. It was a good one, but she still felt agitated. Sensing it, David asked, "What else?"

She gave a helpless shrug of her shoulders. "It's Paul. I—I'm all confused about my feelings for him." She turned her wide brown eyes on David, allowing the pain and hurt to spill out. "I can't seem to get over the hurt." Her voice sounded small to her own ears.

David pressed the tips of his fingers together and watched her intently. "You must let go of your hurt, Julie," he told her softly, firmly. "Lay it down. It's too much for you to carry. Jesus' shoulders are broad enough to carry it all."

"I know that," she said with conviction. "In my head I know that. But in my heart. . . ." She choked back a small cry.

"Julie," David said patiently. "I've spent a good bit of time with Paul over these past weeks."

She looked up, surprised. "He's a fine man, Julie. And frankly, he's very mature in his walk with God."

A bitter taste rose in her mouth and twisted her lips. "How much simpler it would have been if he'd been so mature all along," her voice trailed, stumbling over some private image. "Do you know how much I used to beg him to become a part of my church life?"

"Yes," David responded. And that surprised her, too. He continued, "You know, Julie, you can't *make* someone a Christian by nagging him into the kingdom of God."

Her ire rose. "Is that what he said? That I nagged him about going to church with me?"

David laughed softly, his eyes warm and perceptive. "He didn't have to. Let's say I guessed it." David sobered. "But God comes to a person in His own timing. Not ours. It's an error many ardent Christians make. They're committed. They're on fire for the Lord." David clamped his fist to emphasize his points. "They try to drag loved ones into their circle of joy."

"That's wrong?"

"More of a 'turn off,' I'd say," came David's reply. "It's all right to witness. In fact, we have an obligation to witness," he emphasized. "But God does the leading." His words recalled similar ones her mother had spoken to her on Julie's wedding day so long ago. Had she done that to Paul? Had she been pious and self-righteous? Had she alienated him instead of reflecting to him what Christ meant to her?

She conceded the point. "All right. I see what you mean. But, David . . ." her voice grew grave and low, "there was no justification for what he did to me. None at all." Her back grew rigid as the old memories drifted up from the crevices of her mind. She forced them away, sweeping the back of her hand over her eyes as if the gesture might erase the ugliness. "I'll stick it out with the youth group, David. I promise you that. But that's all I can promise for now." Then she rose and left.

"Julie! You just have to say yes! I mean, Mom can't take me. Rob's being a pain. I have no one else. Please say yes!" Cindy's excited voice cut through the fog in Julie's sleep-stunned brain.

"Christmas shopping? Cindy, give me a break. It's 8:00 on a Saturday morning. I wanted to sleep in. . . ."

Cindy interrupted, "Christmas is only three weeks away. That's twenty-one short days. I have scads of stuff to buy! Please, help me out."

Julie eyed her clock radio balefully. Three weeks! Was that true? She had already done most of her shopping. She'd found a Bible commentary for her dad and several lovely items for her mom in Pennsylvania Quaker country the previous summer. And she'd knitted several small gifts for Cindy, Tess, and her Aunt Christine. *I'm ready for Christmas*, she thought. Why wasn't Cindy?

Yet she could tell from the sound of her voice that the girl would not be put off. "Oh, all right," Julie grumbled.

Cindy squealed with delight. "You're a lifesaver! Let's go to Tyson's Corners." She named one of the largest malls in the Washington area. "Pick me up so we can start the second they open the doors. We'll make a day of it," Cindy bubbled. "I'll even buy you lunch at the Yogurt Bar!"

"Thanks, Big Spender," Julie grumbled.

Together, Cindy chattered endlessly and, in spite of herself, Julie began to warm to the day of shopping. The mall was beautiful inside, decorated in the reds and greens of the season. An enormous tree stood in the center of the mall, where a local radio station was doing a promotional. Buy a Christmas angel to hang on the tree, and the money would go for toys and food for needy families.

One of the larger department stores was a wonderland in white and blue. Large gleaming artificial snowflakes, suspended from the ceiling and a mammoth tree, white and shimmering, attracted wide-eyed kids in large numbers. A toy train, loaded with bright foil-wrapped packages, ran around a track beneath the tree through a community of elves and fairies and reindeer. Julie watched the children's beautiful, awed faces, feeling a yearning she couldn't quite shake.

"Julie," Cindy's voice interrupted her thoughts. "I need some help from you in picking out a very special gift."

Julie focused on the teen's heart-shaped face and luminous green eyes. "For whom? Your mom? Jud?"

"Oh no, those are a cinch. But the youth group collected money for gifts, and I volunteered to buy them."

"You want me to pick out my own gift?" Julie asked, bewildered.

"Of course not, silly!" Cindy flashed Julie her dimpled smile. "I already got yours! I need suggestions from you on what to get Mr. Shannon."

Julie's stomach gave a lurch as she struggled to keep her feelings from registering on her face. "Why me?" she asked, suspiciously.

Cindy's wide eyes scanned her innocently. "Because you knew him in college," she explained with a shrug. "I thought you might remember what he liked."

"Paul Shannon. No fair." Julie's eyes glowed over the beautiful leather-bound book she held in her hands. "You

90

said we couldn't afford a bunch of gifts and now you turn up on Christmas Eve with this." She tried to sound miffed, but her delight over the volume of poetry she held belied her pout.

"So sue me," he chuckled, watching her as she ran her slim, delicate fingers over the inlaid surface of the book. "I saved for weeks," he admitted. "But it was worth every missed lunch."

Her eyes rose to embrace his. "The Love Sonnets of Elizabeth Barrett Browning. Thank you! Oh, Paul, I love you so much!" She hugged him impulsively, throwing her arms around his neck and clutching him with child-like abandon. "Our first Christmas," she mused. "I hope we have a million more!"

He laughed aloud, delighted with her child-woman expression. "We'll be pretty old after a million Christmases. Just two old married people rocking away under their Christmas tree," he said and brushed his hand down the side of her cheek. She shivered and blushed, suddenly self-conscious under his gaze.

"I—I got something for you, too. . . ."

"Julie," he admonished softly.

"Turn about's fair play," she said with a smug expression. She hurried to their bedroom and emerged shortly with a large bulky package. He tore off the paper and found the ivory colored cable-knit sweater she'd knitted for him. "I did it myself, I hope it fits."

He pulled it on over his head. It snugged perfectly across his shoulders, hugged his lean torso, and extended to his waist. But the sleeves ended three inches above his wrists. Awkwardly, they stared at the shrunken sleeves. "It doesn't fit!" Julie cried in horror. Quick tears sprang to her brown eyes. "Oh, Paul! I wanted it to be perfect! And it doesn't fit!"

He dropped quickly next to her on the sofa and gathered her in his arms. "I—I'll f—fix i—it," she mumbled between disappointed tears.

"Don't touch it."

91

"But it doesn't fit!" she cried, turning tear-stained lashes to his face.

Paul caught her chin and tilted it upward to meet his descending mouth. *"I'll get my arms surgically altered,"* he whispered in the space of time it took to capture her lips with his. . . .

"Julie! Julie . . . are you listening to me?" Cindy's question dragged Julie into the present where she blushed furiously.

"I'm sorry, Cindy!"

"I just thought that since you knew Mr. Shannon in college, you might know something special he'd like from us kids." Cindy put her hands on her corduroy clad hips in exasperation. "Don't you have *any* ideas?"

Julie sighed and gathered her wits, concentrating on Cindy's question. "Not really," she said slowly. "But if we put our heads together, I'm sure we'll come up with something."

They ended up buying Paul a leather bookcover for his Bible at a Christian bookstore in the mall. It was a beautiful piece of hand-tooled work, imprinted with the shape of a dove in a rich cordovan color. "Yum!" Cindy said with delight after they'd chosen it. "Don't you just love the smell of real leather? Oh, Julie, this is perfect. I know Mr. Shannon will love it! I know I did the right thing in asking you to help me pick something out for him! I can't wait till he opens it at the Christmas party!"

Julie listened to Cindy's effervescent patter while the sales clerk bagged their purchase. Privately, she marveled at how the simple act of buying a Christmas gift could have filled her with such sadness and longing. Of how she could feel so hollow inside in a time when the world glittered with the lights and the sounds and the smells of the Yule season. Of how her past dogged her present like an avenging angel!

The advertising agency decided to hold the annual Christmas office party on a private yacht, anchored picturesquely in the Potomac. Since the staff was small, the entire group, including spouses and dates, found themselves comfortable and pampered on the luxurious boat. Julie was no exception. She'd come with Van, and together they dined and walked the decks of the vessel.

The December night was cold, but thus far winter had been mild—no snow or ice storms. The stars twinkled above in the black sky and a full moon cut a silvery swath across the dark expanse of the calm river. The boat had sailed briefly before dropping anchor. Julie hugged her arms to herself as she watched the lights twinkle and wink from the faraway shoreline.

"The lady's going to freeze to death," Van's warm voice whispered in her ear as he leaned beside her.

She turned her eyes to him and conceded, "Probably. But I think I've had enough partying for the night. Thanks for freezing out here with me."

He draped his arm around her shoulders and pulled her to nestle under his arm against the warmth of his coat. "It's my pleasure," he murmured in her ear. Her perfume and his cologne mingled and Julie sighed deeply, allowing herself to snuggle for just a moment. It felt good to be held.

From inside, she heard the sounds of music and laughter from her colleagues, ever conscious that she didn't feel part of the festivities. Why did she feel so estranged from everything? The yacht was beautiful, decorated in greens and lavenders and white, aglow with wreaths and holly and bayberry candles. The buffet had been delicious, caviar and meatballs, bite-size delicacies of lobster and shrimp and king crab, and desserts of chocolate fondue-dipped fruit and frothy cream concoctions. The music was soft and romantic. And Van was with her all evening, as always, gracious and charming and tender. But something was missing. Julie knew it, but she couldn't name it.

"I have something for you, Julie." Van's voice dragged her out of her introspection. "I wanted to give it to you tonight."

Surprised, she pulled back and waited as he reached into his jacket pocket and pulled out an oblong box, wrapped in green foil.

Immediately, she reacted. "Oh, Van. No. You shouldn't have. . . ."

"It's Christmas," he chided. "You're a beautiful woman. Men should be buying you foolish, extravagant things. Take it. Please."

Her heart hammered, but she cautiously took the box and gingerly unwrapped it, all the while admonishing herself for allowing herself to lead him on. She liked Van. He was a wonderful man. But. . . . The paper fell away and Julie lifted the lid on the satin-lined box. Inside lay a necklace of simple gold. From its center dangled a small star sapphire. The stone caught the moonlight and the white star, buried in its interior, leaped with a life of its own. The irony of his choice in jewels wrenched at her heart.

"Van . . ." her voice cracked.

"Let me put it on you."

The moment of truth had come. Julie gritted her teeth and looked him squarely in the face. "No. Please, I—I can't take it." Her hand slipped to her throat to halt the attachment of the chain.

"But why, Julie? I want you to have it." His voice sounded hurt, confused.

"Van. . . ." She struggled to control her voice. "I—I just can't. Please understand. I like you. A lot. But. . . ." Her voice failed her.

Van dropped his shoulders slightly with a sign of resignation and turned back to the rail, staring out across the dark and rippling water. "But you don't love me," he finished.

"No," she confessed miserably. Why had she started dating him in the first place? Hadn't all her instincts told her that they'd eventually reach this point? Julie felt a wave of self-loathing pass through her. "Van," her voice was soft as she touched his arm lightly, "I can't give you what you want. I should have never let it go this far. I'm sorry."

A wry smile curved the corners of his mouth. "I have no regrets, Julie. And I guess I've known we were headed this way for sometime now," he admitted. "I kept hoping you'd learn to care about me. But a man knows, Julie. I just wanted you so bad, that . . . well . . . I kept trying to make something happen between us."

"It—it's not you, Van. It's me," she offered. "I— I just don't want to make any commitments."

Van straightened and lifted her chin with his forefinger. The moonlight glanced off his hair, sending golden glints through it. "Ah—Julie Kreel. You're the one I couldn't have," he mused, allowing a smile of resignation to soften his eyes and mouth. "I'll miss you, Julie." He shook his head slightly. "Friends?" he ventured.

She smiled, too, suddenly feeling lighthearted and oddly unencumbered. "Friends," she affirmed.

"All right, friend," he said with a forced lightness to his words, "if we stand out here much longer, we'll freeze in this position. Not that I mind, of course."

"Then let's go inside. I wouldn't want us to turn into icicles." Her smile was bright and relieved, both tender and grateful.

Van took her hand, but he hesitated and added thoughtfully, with a perception that made Julie shiver from far more than the cold night air. "You know who I'd like to get my hands on?" he asked philosophically. "I'd like to meet the guy who caused you to erect this wall around your heart. What a fool he was! To have let you get away."

She said nothing, but slipped her arm around Van's waist and walked with him in the newfound camaraderie into the gaily lit stateroom where the party continued.

CHAPTER 7

JULIE HAD LOOKED FORWARD to the youth caroling night and Christmas party with both anticipation and dread. With anticipation, because it was fun to pile into the hay strewn floor of three pick-up trucks and drive through the Washington suburbs, singing the familiar carols of the season. And with dread, because Paul would be near her all evening long.

She glanced at the wall clock in her apartment, nervously. Why had she ever agreed to let him come and pick her up? She should have insisted on driving her own car to the church parking lot to rendezvous with the kids and trucks. But, no, she had let Paul talk her into riding with him. "Just to cut down congestion in the parking lot," he had said. At the time, it had made sense. But now, fifteen minutes from his arrival, it seemed like a bad idea.

She didn't want Paul in her apartment. It was unreasonable; but, nevertheless, it was how she felt. Her home was her last bastion against his unwanted presence in her life. He'd already invaded her work domain, her church, the lives of her best friends. In fact, Paul's essence lingered like a cloud over every aspect of her life. "There is no memory of him here," she told herself over and over again as she prepared for the evening, then paled at the realization that her thoughts alone had brought him into the room with her.

He arrived, and forcing a calmness into her body that she did not feel, Julie let him inside. "Hi," he flashed her a smile that lit up his blue eyes as he impacted the room with his sound, his scent, his existence.

She watched as he scanned the apartment with photographic eyes, taking in the bits and pieces and details that had been hers and hers alone. "You're early." It was all she could manage as she watched him invade her privacy, her almost five years of tedious reconstruction, her weeks and months and years of metamorphosis from Julie Shannon to Julie Kreel. She was a butterfly forced back into a dark cocoon.

He knew her mind. "Thank you for letting me come here," he told her. "I know you didn't have to. But I'm glad you did." He wore jeans and a bulky shetland sweater beneath a pea jacket of navy blue. It made his eyes seem bright and glowing, like a beacon. She grabbed her own coat, laid hastily over the back of her sofa, but he made no move to help her don it and leave.

Instead, he crossed to the corner of the room that contained her Christmas tree. "It's beautiful," he said, thrusting one hand into his pocket. Julie swallowed, nervous, anxious to be off—away from this room and his magnetic presence. He was taller than the tree and he fingered the short-needled fir with absentminded lingering. "Remember our first tree?" She did. "You insisted that we go out in the woods and cut it ourselves. It took me thirty minutes with an axe that was as dull as a bread knife. You kept telling me, 'It's so small and short, Paul. . . .' " His voice painted the nostalgic picture on her mind's canvas.

Involuntarily, the corners of her mouth turned up.

97

"And when we got it home, it was so tall that you had to cut off two feet from the top."

"And it was frozen solid . . ."

". . . and had to thaw in the bathtub overnight."

"And we bought that bag of cranberries and popped all that popcorn to string into a garland . . ."

". . . and you ate so much of the popcorn that I had to re-pop a batch so we could finish it . . ."

"And I made a star out of an old aluminum can."

They stopped reminiscing, breathlessly, awkwardly. Julie was acutely aware of the warmth that had crept over her body as the pungent fragrance of pine resin drifted upward from the tree, sharp and tangy. The memories had been good. And so vivid. After all this time . . . still so very vivid. Their gazes collided through the branches, tripped over silver and green glass ornaments, then dropped to the carpet below. Abruptly, she cleared her throat, turned, snatched her coat and said, "Let's go. I—I don't want to hold up the party."

He reached for her coat, but she struggled into it, refusing his aid, fighting to regain her composure and reestablish a distance between them. With resolve and recrimination, she dropped a curtain on the stage of their past.

Stupid! she berated herself. *Why did I ever agree to let him come here? Stupid!* "I'm ready," she told him aloud, crossing hurriedly to the door.

She warned him with her eyes, *Stay back! Get away from me!* He allowed her to open the door, standing aside, offering no assistance. Julie fairly flung it open. He followed cautiously, warily, careful to give her plenty of space.

Outside, the night air was frigid and reviving. Julie breathed it in with great gulps, refreshing her mind with its icy reality. Paul opened the door of his sleek black car and she climbed in quickly. They drove in silence to the church and the parking lot where the kids and the trucks and the laughter and the fun of this other time, this other place, awaited them.

"I think we're ready to roll!" David Wilson greeted them from among a cluster of capped, bobbing heads. "Who's got the guitars?"

Four kids brandished their instruments and Paul directed, "All right, make sure you each get into separate trucks. That way we can all have music."

Sharon Wilson snuggled against her husband's chest and allowed her teeth to chatter. David hugged her to him and joked, "Is this the former 'Let's-build-a-snowman-so-what-if-it's-10-below' queen?"

"Your fault!" she said. "You got me used to hearth and home and now I have no tolerance for this weather anymore."

"Well, let me help you into the truck, my dear, and I'll guarantee to find a way to warm you up."

She slugged him playfully. "David Wilson! And you a man of the cloth! I'm shocked."

Their lighthearted banter tugged nostalgically at Julie. It took an act of will to keep her eyes on them and off Paul. Tess took Julie's arm and Julie turned, grateful for the distraction. "Are you coming?"

"No way," Tess said. "A few of us less hardy types will set the goodies out and get ready for the party when you all return. I promise a mug of hot apple cider will be waiting."

The groups began to pile onto the beds of the trucks, shuffling around in the hay. Tess tugged Julie's arm again. "Do me a favor?" Julie nodded. "Keep an eye on Cindy and Jud. I worry about their hormones getting overactive."

Julie glanced at where the couple stood, holding hands and exchanging starry-eyed gazes. Off to herself stood Tina, looking forlorn and left out. Rob hung back, among the stragglers, but Paul was next to him and quickly lured Rob into conversation. They climbed onto the lead truck. Julie followed Cindy and Jud onto the second one. The Wilsons sandwiched themselves onto the third and soon the entire caravan pulled out of the lot and began to wind slowly through the streets.

Julie nestled into the sweet-smelling hay, filling her lungs with the fresh, musky aroma. Overhead, the stars winked down and the street lamps passed like a long row of soldiers in front of home after home. The guitars somehow managed to find a note of mutuality and the clear, distinct voices of youth filled the sharp night air with the familiar ageless beauty of "It Came Upon a Midnight Clear," "Joy to the World," "O Little Town of Bethlehem," and "Silent Night." As the trucks snaked their way through the quiet residential streets, porch lights flickered on and curious residents ventured out to wave and wish the singers a "Merry Christmas."

The homes looked warm and mellow, glowing with colored lights from without and within. Doors wore wreaths, and window after window displayed a variety of beautifully decorated trees. Julie watched and sang with growing peacefulness. This was Christmas as she remembered it. This was the Christmases of her youth, her childhood. It was home and holly and pine and bayberry candles. It was the melodies of ancient carols, the message of long-ago angels, the brightness of a star-studded heaven. It was the season of promise. From birth would come death. From the grave would come resurrection. The story always began with Christmas. Her heart swelled with the emotion of the memories and the music.

The voices from the first truck rose and blended with the voices from her truck. Her ear honed in on Paul's instinctively. His deep baritone filled her hearing until it was all she heard. Automatically, without direction, her own soprano reached to complement his voice, until they had created a harmony that other singers followed with ease.

When they arrived back at the church, the singers poured off the trucks, laughing and slapping their arms, stamping their feet and shouting for cookies and cider. "This way, troops!" David called and led the carolers into the fellowship hall. Julie slipped into the warmth of the lighted hall, transformed in their absence into a party room by many helping hands.

The spicy smells of warm cider and cinnamon rose from a table of homemade delights at one end of the hall. Amid the chatter, laughter, and banter, Julie took her place in one of the two lines that formed on either side of the dessert table.

"That was fun, wasn't it?" Paul asked from behind her in the line.

She nodded, picked up a bright green paper plate, and plodded along behind Tina, scanning the trays of cookies, cakes, and candies, trying hard to focus on the food and not on Paul.

"Hey," Paul said in her ear.

She turned, keeping her body tense, her voice cool. "Hey, what?" she asked suspiciously.

"Hey, you've got hay in your hair," he said, his blue eyes dancing mischievously.

In spite of herself, Julie felt her mouth twitch into a smile. He was so charming. Always so very charming. Something began to thaw inside of her. How could she keep up her barricade of anger and indifference? The truth was, Paul still affected her. His wit, his charm, his disarming smile.

He tugged the pieces of straw from out of her thick hair, careful not to touch her hair, only the hay. "Thanks," she mumbled. At the table, she watched him survey the abundant supply of rich desserts. She knew he'd take the peanut butter balls. They'd eaten a lot of peanut butter together. . . . She knew he'd take two pieces of fudge. And she knew he'd pass over the divinity. He hated the chewy fruit in it.

Without thinking, he picked up the last blueberry tart on a large platter and slipped it onto her plate. Their eyes met and he communicated apologetically over the action. Tastes—likes and dislikes—each remembered the other's. He telepathed a silent "I'm sorry," and she sent him an "It's all right."

Julie sat with the Wilsons, listening to their small

talk. Paul settled across the room, next to Rob. The Freytags arrived to a chorus of welcomes. Mary joined Sharon and soon they were lost in talk. Yes, baby Joshua was holding his own. No, still no word on when he'd be able to come home. Yes, Mary went to the hospital three times a day to touch him, stroke him, fondle him while he lay in his incubator. Julie listened, sharing Mary's concern, forcing her own problems out of her mind.

David gathered the group together after the food had vanished and they filed over to the Christmas tree in the fellowship hall. He riffled through the pile of inexpensive gag gifts and began dispersing them according to their nametags.

Someone gave Jud a pair of toy handcuffs. Another gave Cindy the key and a "No Trespassing!" sign. Rob got a model car kit of a Ferrari. Tina got a toy telephone, jabbing at her reputation for prolonged phone conversations. Julie's heart hammered slightly as Paul unwrapped his gift and felt satisfaction when she saw his genuine surprise and pleasure over the gift. She opened hers, only to stare flustered at a leather bound volume of poetry, slim and expensive. Her heart lurched and she mumbled "Thank you," all the while avoiding Paul's eyes.

Cindy bubbled on about how she hoped Julie liked it and so Julie smiled, reining in her emotions tightly, suddenly wishing the party would end and she could go home. Except that she'd come with Paul. Panicking, she leaned over and arranged with Tess for a ride home and then when everyone began to leave, Julie slipped outside to say goodbye to them and wish a round of "Merry Christmases" with a gaiety she did not feel.

Julie felt as forlorn and wind-swept as the now empty parking lot, lit with the artificial brilliance of mercury vapor lamps. She stamped her feet against the effects of the cold and tugged her collar tightly over her throat.

"I'm sorry, Julie," Paul's voice came to her through the shadows and then he was standing in front of her, staring down, the harsh light of the street lamp cutting sharp patterns across his angular face. "I say that a lot to you, don't I?"

"You picked out the book, didn't you?" she asked without rancor. She knew the answer.

"Cindy asked me for a suggestion. I gave her the idea. But she chose the book," he explained, awkwardly, apologetically. "I didn't mean for it to unnerve you."

Julie shrugged and let out a long sigh. She was suddenly so tired; so drained. "It's a lovely book. Really. You don't have to apologize."

"Do you want me to take you home now?"

It was her turn to feel awkward. "I—I asked Tess to take me."

Silence separated them like a wall. She raised her eyes to his face. His own eyes were hooded and guarded. He kept his hands jammed deep in his coat pockets and a cold, maverick wind gusted, lifting his dark curls and scattering them on his forehead.

"Well . . ." he started, "what will you do for Christmas?"

"I'm taking a few days off and flying to Columbus to be with Mom and Dad."

"How are they?"

"Fine. . . ." She smiled, softening her guard.

"Tell them 'Hello' for me."

"Sure. And you, Paul? What will you do on Christmas Day?" Strangely, it mattered to her that he didn't have to spend Christmas alone. No one should be alone on Christmas.

"My folks are touring the West in a camper trailer they bought two years ago," he explained. "I can't get vacation time off from the firm anyway. David Wilson has invited me to spend the day with him and Sharon and the kids, so I'll go there."

"Good," Julie said sincerely. The cold permeated her coat and her teeth chattered. She needed to go inside and find Tess. But she was somehow reluctant to leave, oddly torn between leaving him and staying near him. *Why? It's the season,* she told herself. *It's just because it's Christmas.*

"Well . . ." Paul said, lagging and lingering in the bitter cold night. "I guess this is it till after the holidays."

"I—I guess so," she confirmed. A halo of light surrounded his head. A shadow tracked his cheekbone from the outside edge of his eye to the corner of his full, provocative mouth.

"I'll call you before New Year's."

No! Don't! her mind cried. "Sure. That'll be fine," her voice said.

Paul stepped back. "Merry Christmas, Julie," he whispered, his voice so low that she had to lean forward to catch his words in the wind. Then he turned and walked quickly to his car. It looked metallic and burnished by the street lamp, a black-gold metal animal, poised for flight. She watched him drive away, an aching inside her that hung, clinging like the cold, damp and deep and lonely.

"Merry Christmas, Paul," she said to the empty night.

The quiet of the dusty top floor of the law library settled around Julie as she struggled to keep her mind on her job. Outside, it was a brilliant October day, dazzling and splendid, adorned with reds and golds and browns, the sky a brilliant, searing blue and the air fresh and tingling with the crisp smells of autumn. And Julie was stuck in the library amid the dust and the clutter and the dead air.

Idly, she fingered the cart of antique volumes that had to be reshelved; old and outdated books that were no longer used in modern, more advanced times, but too unique and unusual to be thrown away or discarded.

Memories of the night before filled her mind like bitter dregs. She and Paul had fought. Again. It seemed to be a way of life with them anymore. He split his time be-

tween his job on the campus and his job as a law clerk with the Rinaldi firm. He was ambitious and qualified. He would move up quickly within the firm. Julie knew it and the idea frightened her. It seemed the higher he climbed professionally, the worse their marriage fared.

She had given her notice at the law library. With Paul's extra income, she could finally quit the job she'd loathed for so long. But now, the act seemed extraneous. Why quit, when there was nothing for her at home?

For some reason, the books were especially heavy and Julie could hardly lift them to the shelves. And the dust clung to her hands and settled in her throat, making it feel parched and dry. Dead. That's how she felt. Dead and dusty and worn out . . . just like the old books.

She wandered over to the window, gazing out into the sunlit courtyard of the campus below. The dust and grime lay heavily on the windowsill. Absently, Julie wiped a pane of glass with her palm. Small smudge marks smeared the grime, but the sunlight struggled through and added to her melancholia and loneliness.

Outside a phenomenon of nature had occurred. It was raining—a fine misting sprinkle that descended to the grass and sidewalks and trees below. Yet the sun still shone. It sliced through the rain, causing each droplet to reflect the sun's shimmering rays. The shower fell like a curtain of fine gold, like golden dust, like a golden veil of sun-shot wetness.

Students scurried for the protective coverings of doorways, huddling to wait out the brief and glittering shower. A movement caught Julie's eye. A movement of intimacy. Of one couple, huddled together in a doorway, their bodies bent close, almost clinging to ward off the slanting spray of rain.

Something caught in Julie's throat. The familiar body of the man, his dark curling hair damp, leaned protectively over the woman. She was lithe and tawny, gold colored, like the rain. She dipped her head toward the man's chest. He touched her hair, brushing off the rain-

drops, letting his hands smooth over the shoulders of her black linen business suit.

A sudden chill went over Julie. A chill that originated from within, that snaked down her arms and legs and left her weak and trembling. As suddenly as it had come, the rain stopped. And the beautiful couple, the lean-limbed man and the lion-colored woman moved out of the doorway, crossed quickly to the street and got into the woman's silver automobile—a Jaguar.

A cat should own a cat, Julie observed stoically, too numb, too stricken to think anything else. Yes, the car fit Bianca Rinaldi. Silver and gold. Jaguar and lioness. Man and woman.

Julie did not finish shelving the books. Instead, she walked down to the first floor, calmly removed her coat from the closet, gathered up her purse and some personal items and walked out of the library. Out into the clean, rain-washed October day. Out into the rain-soaked grass and sun-dappled leaves. She never went back.

"You look like you've lost your best friend, Julie," David found Julie sitting pensively in the fellowship hall, waiting for Tess who was cleaning up in the kitchen.

Julie smiled wanly and watched as he settled next to her on a metal chair. "Want to tell me about it?" he asked.

"You have the kindest eyes," she blurted, then blushed, ashamed at the observation.

He laughed and his eyes crinkled at the corners. "And you have the saddest eyes," he countered. "Come on—it's Christmas."

"I'm glad you're having Paul over on Christmas Day."

David nodded, understanding. "So it's Paul."

She blushed, feeling vulnerable and exposed. "I wish I could get him out of my life," she said, without much conviction or fire. "But he's changed, David. He truly has."

"What do you think God wants, Julie?" David asked, causing her to jerk her full attention to him. Instantly, she felt her defenses go up.

"Paul and I made our choices years ago, David. We can't go back."

"That's true," David observed. "But you can go forward. Christ calls His people to be reconciled to one another. Without reconciliation, we are impotent as a body. Useless for the work of the Spirit."

"Reconciled?" she gasped. "You can't mean remarriage?"

He held up his hand to ward off her outburst. "No. That's between you and Paul and God. But as your pastor, I need to tell you that you must reconcile your differences as Christians, as human beings. You and Paul have work to do in this church. God's placed you here together to accomplish something for Him. You can't keep fighting those purposes. You can't function as a team, with animosity and strife between you."

The truth of his words pierced her. "And the past is a wedge that is separating us from God. Is that what you're saying?"

David smiled and covered her hands with his. He looked intently into her eyes, "Yes, it is. Your past hurts are being used by Satan to undermine the good that the two of you can accomplish for these kids. Divorced or not. Like it or not. First and foremost, you're Christians. And if you're under Christ's banner, you must be reconciled."

"And you'll be our arbitrator?" she asked, a tinge of resignation creeping into her voice.

"If you'll let me, yes, I will," David said. "But in the meantime, open yourself to God and stop fighting Him." An impish smile curved on his mouth. "Go with the flow."

Julie giggled. "I don't remember that verse in the Bible."

David shrugged and let his tone grow serious again.

"Julie, pray about reconciliation. It's God's answer for healing."

That night, Julie lay for a long time, contemplating David's words. He was right, of course. She could not harbor her hurt and resentment against Paul and still function productively in the church or the youth group. And her admission that Paul was somehow different had been honest and heartfelt.

Still, she could not allow him back into her life. She couldn't see into the future and couldn't guess what God intended for her and Paul. She intended distance and isolation. She intended to insulate herself against the devastating effects of Paul Shannon on her mind and her body, and now her spirit. Perhaps it was time to find out what God intended. She took a long shuddering breath and promised to turn the situation over to Him.

CHAPTER 8

JULIE RETURNED TO WASHINGTON and her job feeling refreshed and revitalized after the Christmas holidays. She'd enjoyed returning to her childhood home, relaxing with the familiar surroundings of Mom's cooking and Dad's ever-present Christmas movie camera. Her parents had seemed pleased to learn that Paul was now in Washington and that Julie had managed to make a peace within herself about it. She hadn't realized before how hard her divorce had been on both of them.

It was this attitude of benevolence that allowed her to talk to Paul, lightly, without the old hurts of the past sandwiched between their conversation when he called her at her office. His law firm was having a New Year's Eve party and would Julie please come with him.

At first, she balked. Surely there were other women he could take. No, he'd said. He wanted her to come. Please. It wasn't a big event, simply a small party among the higher echelon of the firm. Breathlessly, she agreed, then spent three days shopping for something to wear, not because she didn't have an evening dress but because she wanted something *very* special. She didn't know why. She just wanted to be beautiful and sexy and glamorous.

"Fickle," she told Tess expansively. "Fickle and foolish and unpredictable. That's what I am."

"No," Tess said to her. "It's called being a woman."

Julie spent far too much money on a dress of black velvet, studded subtly with minute stones that caught the light and glimmered whenever she moved. The sleeves were long, the neckline, a deep-V, allowing the creamy expanse of her throat and skin to show provocatively. She piled her hair, Gibson Girl fashion, on her head and surveyed the effect in her mirror. She pronounced the effort worthwhile.

The look on Paul's face when he saw her confirmed her appraisal. She thought him truly elegant in the trappings of formal black tie, complete to the ice blue ruffled shirt. The suit fitted across his shoulders perfectly, impeccably. His dark hair curled in tight clusters; his blue eyes, accentuated by the blueness of his shirt, pierced through her like darts.

They arrived at the modern skyscraper after a long wait in snarled traffic, while the city prepared to turn out the old year and bring in the new. They elected to take the outside glass elevator to the penthouse supper club on the 95th floor. Julie watched, breathlessly, as the city fell away during the ascent into the inky blackness of the night. The lights of the city sparkled and blinked, stretching out as far as her eye could see, giving the area a shimmering aura that arched into the night and hovered above the city like a bird with opened wings.

The supper club was an understated collection of polished wood, pecan veneers, and selected antiques. It reminded her of an English barrister's domain, except that one entire wall was glass and looked out over the city and the meandering Potomac River. The Capitol building, the Washington Monument, the White House, stood out, haloed and lighted, laid like precious stones against the darker countryside.

Paul introduced her to his colleagues as, "Julie Kreel, a friend." She relaxed with the men and their wives, focused on their shop talk, their snips of personal history and animated versions of plea bargaining. She felt like Cinderella, extricated from the complexities of her life and brought by Prince Charming to this place of neutrality, this Ball of Gentility and Graciousness.

They ate and laughed and danced together, suspended in the atmosphere between the night and the dawn. Here the world was different; her feelings uncluttered by the trappings of yesterday. Here, there was no past, no future, only the present—the now.

Paul guided her to the dance floor and she drifted into his arms as a leaf on water. It was as if the cells of her body had a memory of their own, independent from her mind . . . a will, a life force she could not consciously control. They remembered what her mind would not. The feel of his arms encircling her, the pressure of his hand on hers, the distance between the top of her head and the bottom of his chin when he held her. They remembered all of it. Every nuance, every pattern laid down by intimate habit. Symbiosis. Separate organisms . . . yet together. Paul and Julie. . . .

A mirrored sphere spun slowly above them as they danced. Its myriad facets of glass caught and reflected the room's light and sent it reeling off the dancers below. Glints of light pricked her vision, glanced over Paul's hair and shoulders, tangled in his hair, bounced off his cheekbones. Shards of light that sliced and exposed her heart to a bittersweet yearning.

His eyes glowed with an intensity that caused her breath to quicken and her blood to race. His nearness aroused some old and ancient fire that smoldered beneath the surface of her breeding, the layer of her refinement.

From somewhere outside their circle of dancing light, she heard the haunting strains of "Old Lange Syne" and then streamers and confetti fell, like colored rain. They stopped dancing, stood motionless amid the laughter and music and the people surrounding them, alone in a universe of their own making. The rhythm of their pulses flowed together. The power of their unity bound them tightly.

"Happy New Year," Paul told her, his eyes intense, compelling. And she found herself drowning in the blueness of his eyes as his mouth descended down . . . down to touch hers . . . filling her with an unquenchable longing and lifting her up . . . up to the peaks of a mountain she had not climbed in five years.

The kiss was as natural as breathing, as unplanned as her next heartbeat. The pressure of his lips on hers was tantalizing, teasing, leaving her with a gnawing, primitive hunger for more. And Julie was filled, inexplicably, with an emotion somewhere between wonderment and fear.

"You could go with me if you wanted to, Julie," Paul's anger kindled the air causing her to flinch, but not to stop the motions of her packing.

She drew in her breath, resigned, and continued to lay clothing in the interior of her suitcase. "I told my boss I'd go to the conference for the agency and I'm going," she said, stubbornly. "I have a job, too, you know, and as long as I have to work, the least I can do is give them their money's worth."

"Look, this party is very important to me, Julie. Rinaldi himself invited me and I want you there with me." He tried to reason, to compromise with her.

Her lips twisted into a bitter line. "Your new friends will be there, Paul. What could I possibly contribute to your rise to the top at Rinaldi?" The acid in her voice dripped over the word "friends" and Paul raked his hand through his hair in exasperation.

"You're not going to start that again, are you?" His tone was sarcastic and angry.

Julie snapped the lid of her suitcase and crossed to her cosmetic table. There she began to load her personal toiletries into her matched overnight case. "It's a three-

day conference," she said tightly. "My plane leaves in two hours. I'll be back late Sunday night. I told the agency I would represent them and I intend to keep my promise. Now if you'll excuse me. . . ." She tried to step around him.

Paul blocked her path, deliberately, taking her shoulders firmly in his hands. His grip was so tight that she winced. "You're hurting me." She struggled to break his hold, but he held her without yielding. Julie looked into his eyes and saw his anger. Her own anger, bedded in stubbornness, rose to clash with his.

His breath came ragged to her ears and for a moment she stood, caught between his fury and her vengefulness, balancing between fear and pride. "All right, Julie. Then go." His voice was stony, controlled. He let go of her arms and stepped backward. She ached where his fingers had bruised, but she didn't flinch.

With deliberation, he took his coat and left the bedroom, leaving the door ajar. She heard him slam outside into the cold November morning and swallowed down her tears of frustration and hurt.

Hurriedly, Julie finished packing and dressing. She told herself that they'd straighten things out when she got home from the business conference. They'd sit down and hash out their differences over his career, the time he spent with Bianca, the loneliness and isolation Julie felt in this world of corporate law and professional ladder climbing. They'd settle their problems over dinner and a warm fire and. . . .

Julie pushed aside the flood of pain and hurt that threatened to engulf her and quickly called a cab to take her to the airport.

For Julie, New Year's Eve marked a beginning of a renewed relationship with Paul. The bond between them was tenuous, grounded in the past on one level, yet structured in the present on another. They didn't speak of their former life with each other, but it tied them together like string around a packet of old love letters.

Cautiously, ever so cautiously, Julie allowed him some access to her life, lowering barriers of resentment and distrust.

Paul responded as one might who'd found a stricken bird with a broken wing. He protected her and nurtured the bud of life that had sprung from the earth of past mistakes. He led her, carefully, away from the complexities of passion into the simplicities of good times, laughter, conversation, and sharing. She accepted his companionship and grew comfortable with it.

They did things with the youth group. They took frequent trips to the city. They attended movies, art gallery showings, took drives into Maryland and western Virginia. They spent a day at Williamsburg, another at Harper's Ferry, and a third at Mount Vernon. And as the weather warmed, turning the winter into spring, Julie felt a thawing within herself and a peace and contentment bloom that she had not known in years.

"You really look happy," Tess told her one April afternoon as they lunched in a fashionable Georgetown tearoom. "Could those be stars in your eyes?"

Julie locked her fingers together and gave her friend a rueful smile across the pink linen tablecloth. "You're worse than a mother hen, Tess Germaine. Paul and I have had some very good times together these past few months. But don't go getting any ideas about us. Our youth group commitment is the only reason we spend so much time together."

Tess wagged her finger, "Stubborn 'til the end, aren't you Julie? Well, you're about to be tested. I understand that the Freytags brought their baby home yesterday."

"Oh, Tess! That's wonderful!" Julie exclaimed, setting her tea cup into its china saucer. "I'm going to call her and invite myself over for a peek at him. I can't help but remember the first time I saw him . . .

all hooked up to those wires and monitors." She shuddered at the vivid image.

"What I was inferring," Tess continued on her previous track, "was that in a few months you'll be giving up the youth group. Then what will you use for an excuse to see Paul?"

A small cloud crossed Julie's countenance. "Then I guess it will be over."

Tess looked at her skeptically. "You are *so* hardheaded! When are you going to let go and just give yourself over to the man?"

Julie suddenly didn't like the turn of the conversation. It confused and upset her to think of Paul beyond their current pleasant, safe little relationship. She felt she'd done as David had counseled. She'd reconciled with Paul. They had the common ground of the church between them. It was impossible to relate to him beyond that context. "Let's change the subject."

Tess stared at her through her owl-eyed glasses, sighed, and flowed into a new topic. "On a note of maternal relief, it does look like the teen love story of the year is tapering off."

"Cindy and Jud?"

Tess nodded. "Unfortunately, it's more Jud than Cindy. I hate to see her moping around like she is, but I think that Jud's been feeling confined. It's just as well," Tess said through a bite of salad, "Cindy's far too young and far too serious about him."

Julie agreed, knowing firsthand how painful and heartrending first love could be. Paul had been her first love. She could still remember how just his presence in the law library would make her whole day. And how her stomach fluttered if she so much as caught sight of him across the campus. Or how depressed she felt if she'd seen him with another girl in the coffee shop. She had to force herself to not think about the passion he had been able to arouse in her. It had been earth shaking. Soul shattering. She shook her head to clear it. Her thoughts had taken a dangerous course.

115

Physical love was something she would never share with Paul again. She shouldn't dwell on it.

"And Rob?" Julie asked, anxious to emerge from the dark tunnel she'd wandered into mentally.

Tess let out a deep sigh and smiled warmly. "He's like another kid, Praise the Lord. And I have Paul to thank for that. He's managed to get Rob turned around and headed on the right path again. I'll always be grateful for what he's done for my son."

Julie understood. Rob had done a 180 degree turnabout over the winter. Tess articulated Julie's thought. "Somehow, Paul's diffused Rob's anger and helped him to realize that Hank's failure to be a father is not his fault. That Rob isn't to blame for Hank's leaving and his rejection of his family."

Ultimately, Julie realized that Paul's reemergence into her life had been painful, but not all bad. He had touched the lives of people that she cared about, and changed them for the better. It counted. While things would never be the same for her and Paul, it was gratifying to know that something good had risen from the ashes of her hurt and despair.

Julie arrived at the Freytag home the following Saturday. Mary welcomed her with a glowing smile and led her down the hallway of her house to the nursery that sheltered her son. The room sparkled with a circus motif. Bright blues and splashes of yellow adorned the curtains and walls. A clown, hand-painted on one wall, held a cluster of bright balloons. "It's adorable," Julie whispered to Mary, as her eyes roamed the room.

"Here's what all the fuss was about," Mary whispered and led Julie to the side of the glossy white crib. Joshua lay on his stomach in the center of sheets decorated with cartoon lions and circus ponies and elephants, covered over with a lemon yellow afghan. His tiny cheek was pressed against the bed, a fuzz of fine dark hair covering his perfectly formed head.

"He's so beautiful," Julie ached to reach down and touch his sleeping face.

"He'll be up in a few minutes screaming for his bottle. Then you can hold him."

Julie nodded with eager anticipation, then followed Mary back down the hall to the kitchen where she poured them each a cup of coffee.

"He's perfectly fine, isn't he?" Julie asked.

"Perfectly," Mary confirmed. "Thanks to all the prayers and support of the Wilsons and the church. I couldn't have made it without them."

Julie understood. "I—uh—I guess you'll be coming back to the youth group soon," she ventured.

"Not until after the camping trip," she said with a teasing glint in her eye.

Julie rolled her eyes. "You're going to make me do it, aren't you? You're going to make me sleep in a tent for a week."

"You'll love it. Promise," she added when Julie looked askance. "Besides, Don tells me that Paul's an old hand at camping. He did a lot of it during the time he worked with the 'Y.' And," she kidded, "spending a whole week with Paul under the stars isn't *that* bad of a sentence."

Julie dropped her eyes and blushed. Now Mary was doing it, too! Pairing her off with Paul. Mary added, "I've seen the way he looks at you, Julie. He's not exactly immune and indifferent, you know." Julie's discomfort grew. Mary didn't know what she was saying. Of course, she had no idea about herself and Paul.

A thin wail from Joshua's nursery relieved her distress. "Oops!" Mary rose hastily. "The prince is calling for his lunch." Mary opened the refrigerator and pulled out a bottle, set it in a pan on the stove, and turned on the gas jet. "Be a love," she said to Julie as she performed the task. "Go in there and rock him till I get this thing heated."

In the nursery, Julie gingerly picked up the crying infant and cooed softly to him. He screwed up his face

117

and squealed his displeasure. She laughed, deep in her throat, and cuddled him against her breast, carried him to the rocker, and sat down. He was very tiny and so feather light! Julie cradled his head on her arm and traced her finger along the side of his cheek. Greedily, he turned to suckle it.

"Not yet, little fellow." He stopped his wailing and opened his dark brown eyes at her. A concentrated frown puckered his miniature features and Julie felt a longing, as old as time, as powerful as the pulsations of life, surge through her. A baby. A human life. The ultimate testimony of married love. The turning of two halves into a whole. The blending of man and woman to create another living thing.

Joshua fluttered his silky eyelashes and Julie ached for what she could not have. *If only . . . Dear Lord . . . if only. . . .*

Very gently, with great purpose, she laid her cheek next to the baby's, inhaling his fresh powder scent, and let him snuggle against her face under the indifferent gaze of the painted clown.

Julie knew she had to face the realities of the youth camping trip sooner or later. She checked out some books from the library and read about building fires, cooking on open fires, and pitching tents. She learned the difference between a hunter's fire for cooking, a reflector fire for all night heating and warming, a long-burning Indian fire, and a council fire for quiet evenings of storytelling under the stars. She spent hours mulling over photographs of leaves, learning the difference between white oak, red oak, and poison oak. She studied diagrams of knot tying and tent pitching, deciding finally to let Paul figure out some things for the group.

With Paul, she helped plan morning devotions, chose specific Bible passages for prayer and meditation, and memorized a booklet of special camping songs to buoy the group for days of tramping through woods and mountain trails.

"The white water canoe trip will be the highlight," Paul assured her during one planning session at the church. "We'll get the canoes here," he pointed at a dark spot on a map next to a twisting blue line, "paddle to this point," he touched another dot, "carry the canoes around the rapids and turbulence, here, and launch them again here. All in all, we'll cover about fifteen miles worth of river."

Julie smiled wanly and wondered again why she'd ever agreed to such an idea. Camping, indeed!

Fund raising for the expenses of food, gas, and camping gear proved to be a lot more suitable to her talents. Julie organized a car wash, a bake sale, and a rummage sale. The church supported every function gallantly, but an ice cream social and square dance in late May, three weeks before the trip, proved to be the most successful venture of all.

The fellowship hall sported bales of hay, Western posters, and tables with red-checkered cloths lining the parameters of the room allowed plenty of room for square dancing. Julie arrived with Paul, decked out in Western attire of full denim skirt, a fitted red T-shirt, red bandana, and straw hat that hung down her back on a drawstring. She completed her cowgirl image by pulling her long ebony hair into a ponytail and tying a bright red ribbon around it.

"Well, my, my! Ain't you the picture," Paul drawled at her, his blue eyes warm and amused.

"Bet you say that to all the girls!" she said, flirting capriciously with her eyelashes. He looked the part of the modern urban cowboy, in sun-faded jeans, pale blue fitted western shirt with pearl snap buttons, black hat, and leather boots. Her pulse fluttered under his touch.

"Mightin' I have the pleasure of this dance, Miss Kitty?" he asked, bowing from the waist and offering her his arm as the band tuned instruments for the dance.

"Why, sure thing Mr. Dillon." She took his arm and joined a set of three other couples on the dance floor. A fiddler and dance caller began his sing-song calls and soon Julie was swept up in the beat of the dance, her skirt and hair flying as Paul's arms led her through the elaborate instructions.

Paul swung her high off the floor until she was dizzy and leaning against his side for support. She felt his hands on her waist, her hips, her shoulders. She glowed with the exertion, reveled in the physical closeness of him as she laughed and pranced and whirled. She was carefree and flying and full of the music and the intoxicating nearness of Paul.

The room was filled with people. Yet somehow, she saw only Paul. She ate ice cream with the Wilsons, but watched only Paul. She teased and giggled with Cindy and Tina, but danced with only Paul. He was everywhere, filling her vision, her senses, her mind with his presence.

By the time they drove back to her apartment, there was a vibrating undercurrent between them that she sensed, but couldn't quite name. A tension, that fairly crackled with their awareness of one another. Julie snuggled into the glow of that feeling, letting it possess her, wash over her, enfold her.

Inside, she reached for the wall switch, but Paul's hand closed over hers and he said huskily, "Don't."

She trembled, feeling his arms slip around her from behind as he pulled her gently against his chest.

Light from a full moon spilled in through sliding glass doors, bathing the room in a pale ethereal color. Moonlight, shimmering, glowing, swirled on the carpet and sofa in billowing sheets of timelessness. He kissed her exposed neck, leisurely, bringing his lips up the base of her tilted neck to her ear.

He led her over to the pools of moonlight where he turned her slowly in a pirouette, a slow waltz to unorchestrated music played by ghostly moonbeams. She spun for him, a dance of his design, watching the moon's rays highlight the side of his face as she twirled. He stopped her slow spiral and she could almost taste the sweetness of his mouth as he gazed down into her upturned face. The orchestra inside her head tuned her senses, filling her with a heady languid melody played by invisible strings.

Her knees went weak and her heart hammered to the harmony of her longings. Her arms floated upward, around his neck. She rose, lifting her mouth for him, willing him to play her, to stroke her. Again, her body remembered. Again, her flesh responded. She was a being with no will of her own. He had seeped into her very pores . . . soaked into her cells and was floating in her bloodstream.

He lifted her, turned with her, holding her to him, cradling her in his arms. His scent invaded her. She lay her head against his chest. She heard the beat of his heart calling her name. Once again, she bore the indelible stamp of his possession.

"Julie," he whispered her name, "Julie, let me love you."

She could deny him nothing. She was his. He was hers. They were a symphony. "Yes, Paul . . . Yes. . . ." Her words spilled out from a reservoir of longing.

He carried her to the sofa and laid her gently, tenderly on the moon-bathed fabric and then knelt beside her, untying the ribbon from her hair, running his fingers through its thickness, spreading it out in a dark moon-flecked fan. Something stirred at the far end of the sofa. A white furry shape mewed its displeasure over its displacement. Hector.

And for Julie, the pictures came back. Lurid, horrible pictures of another cat in another time. A tawny cat. A lioness. Bianca. Bianca and Paul. A cry, anguished, agonized, tore from her throat and she heaved against Paul's chest with one powerful thrust of rejection.

121

"No!" The word ripped out of her and she scrambled off the sofa, trembling, shaking, tight-fisted, staring at his bewildered expression in the colorless moonlight. "Go away!" She choked out the words. "Don't touch me! I can't stand the thought of you ever touching me again! Not after what you did. I hate you!" She strangled over the last.

Paul stood slowly, drawing in his breath in a long ragged gulp. He backed away from her, his eyes dull and resigned. She watched him cross to the door, while waves of nausea and self-revulsion pounded her psyche. At the door, he gripped the knob, keeping his back to her. "You know, Julie," he said, his voice very low, almost toneless. "I believe that God has forgiven me for what I did. Why can't you?"

He left and the door clicked softly behind him.

CHAPTER 9

SILENCE SETTLED AROUND JULIE like a shroud. A cloud bank covered the moon turning the apartment into a leaden, death-like tomb. Within her, passion metamorphasized into agony and agony into loss. The loss that comes of broken dreams, of brutalized idealism, of corrupted trusts. Once again, she was alone, a prisoner of her own hurt. And her jailer, her tormenter, her persecutor had thrust her into the hell of locked away memories, the torture of a past once buried. Against her will, against her reason, she remembered. . . .

Julie sank against the cool cushion of the taxi and shook her head trying to clear out the weariness and frustration. Paul had been right about the conference. She should have stayed home and gone to the party at his law firm. From the very start, the conference had proven a disaster.

Friday's meetings had been dull and droning. Saturday's had been partially cancelled. Three of the panelists were stranded by bad weather and never arrived. Saturday night's banquet had centered around bad food, a splitting headache, and a pass from an inebriated participant. Yes, her going had been a mistake from the very beginning.

"Well, at least I can salvage Sunday!" Julie had told herself late the night before. She had hurriedly packed at midnight, caught a cab to O'Hare and spent five hours on stand-by until she managed to cath a red-eye special to La Guardia. With the time change, she would be home by 8:00 a.m. Julie looked at her wristwatch. Paul might still be in bed.

"Perfect!" she told herself with an inward smile. She'd slip into the apartment, undress, and slide into bed next to him. She was exhausted. But she didn't want sleep. She wanted her husband next to her. She wanted to feel his warm sleep-laden kisses. She wanted to have him hold her, cuddle her, forgive her for her stubbornness.

The cab pulled up in front of the old brownstone, undistinguished by its crumbly, worn facade. Julie paid the driver, grappled with her luggage and navigated the steps to her front door. A weak November sun struggled through a bank of low gray clouds, making the tree branches look barren and forlorn, dark and spindly.

The neighborhood still slept. Newspapers lay waiting on old, sagging doorsteps. Bikes and toys lay scattered on front stoops. Parked cars lined the silent street, their windshields crusted over with a film of hoarfrost. The sunlight glanced off of something flashy, silver, and Julie dipped her head to shield her tired eyes from the offending glare. From far away, a dog barked.

She entered the apartment quietly, depositing her suitcases next to the sofa, hiking her purse strap higher on the shoulder of her heavy coat to keep it from hitting the floor with a thud. The room was darkened, the curtains still drawn. Good! That meant Paul was asleep. She could sneak into the bedroom and undress and snuggle up next to him, awakening him in her own way, in her own timing. She smiled inwardly at the surprise she'd give him and at the growing desire she felt burgeoning inside of her.

Afterward, they'd brew coffee and she'd make cinnamon toast and they'd talk. They'd clear the air. They'd make peace with each other and begin again—fresh, with renewed outlooks.

Julie opened the bedroom door and stared at the bed and Paul's sleeping body. Curiously, the space in the bed next to him, her space, was not empty. "How odd," she thought, uncomprehending momentarily the tableau before her. Suddenly, for Julie, time stopped. Like a child's kaleidoscope, pictures, frozen, then fluid, swirled in colors of brown and taupe and gray. Paul lay stomach down, the sheet hugging his hips, his back bare and muscular, sinewy and relaxed in the dim brown, filtered light.

A being, brown and cat-like, rose up next to him, her hair, tangled, spilling over tawny shoulders, her eyes gold and kittenish blinking at the intrusion into her den. Paul. Bianca. The picture burned into Julie's mind and from somewhere she heard an audible gasp, a cry, a scream that strangled over the barrier of the truth and died on the field of understanding. The moment in time crystallized, formed a permanent copy on her brain, and solidified in shockwaves that somehow mobilized her legs into action.

She heard someone say, "Oh, my God!" and "Julie! Julie!" and then she ran. She hit the front door with a force that snapped it open with a crack like a cannon. And she ran. Down the quiet residential streets, down the straight old sidewalks, across intersections, weaving a path through parked cars, then moving cars, ignoring the beeping horns, the red lights, the angry gestures of motorists. Julie ran . . . until her lungs felt like bursting, until perspiration poured down her back and off her face, until her legs could no longer support her weight.

Her lungs were on fire. Blackness seemed to close in on her and she stopped against a wall, heaving, shuddering, fighting off nausea and leg cramps. But the picture in her mind would not go away. She saw it again and again. Over and over. A looping replay in colors of

*sepia and brown and umber. Paul asleep, the sheet en-
twined around his hips. And Bianca, raised up on one
elbow with the expression of a cat who'd just lapped a
saucer of warm milk.*

Julie paced the floor of David's office like a caged
animal. It had taken her two days to get up the courage
to come to him. And now that she was here, words
deserted her and all that was left was tension and hot,
raw emotions. Prayer had deserted her. God had abandoned her. She was shamed, angry, shocked at what
had almost happened between herself and Paul. And
the intensity of the pain and the sense of humiliation
his touch had brought back to her.

Her carefully built wall, so painfully constructed over
five years had been blown away with one passionate
moment. Her disgust welled within her, until she finally erupted at the gentle-eyed man who sat behind
his desk, watching her, waiting for her to speak.

"It was a nightmare, David! Don't you see? I can't
ever be friends with Paul. There's too much hurt. The
memories keep coming back!" Tears shimmered in her
eyes and her hands clenched and unclenched. "He—
he betrayed me! And our marriage vows!"

David pressed the tips of his fingers together and
caught Julie's trembling gaze with his. "Don't you think
Jesus knows something about betrayal, Julie?" he asked
quietly. "Don't you think that by becoming a man for
our sakes, He experienced all the same anguish when
one of His disciples sold Him to the high priest and
another denied Him with an oath?"

Julie froze, feeling a warm flush start on her neck.
"Yes, but. . . ."

"Because He understands," David continued, more
forcefully, "only He can take away your pain and hurt.
You have allowed the enemy to revive the past and
dominate your mind with it. By not giving your hurt
over to Christ, you have let the enemy tear apart the
good thing that Paul and you have rebuilt.

"What you have to ask yourself, Julie, is 'Why am I mad?' Because of what happened five years ago? Or because of what you felt for Paul the other night."

Julie's flush deepened. "We—we're divorced," she tried defensively. "He committed adultery! God forbids it and Paul did it. And even God lets people divorce because of it!" she finished, her eyes glittering with hostility.

David shook his sandy brown hair and gave her a smile. "Julie, Christ allowed divorce 'for the hardness of men's hearts,' " David quoted. "He neither advocated nor mandated it."

"But adultery," she stabbed with the word.

"Is sin," David finished. "Paul did it. He knows it. And his sin is between him and God. I know that you got mowed down in the process. Sin's like that. Everybody loses. Look at David in the Old Testament," he said, touching his Bible on top of his desk. "He committed adultery and then tried to rectify it with murder! Yet God still loved him. And forgave him." David emphasized his last words and Julie winced.

"In fact, it was David and Bathsheba who gave Israel Solomon."

"Are you telling me I shouldn't have divorced Paul?" she asked, her voice guarded, her body taut and tight.

David shook his head. "Not at all. Every marriage can't be salvaged. But sometimes divorce is used as a loophole to protect and escape instead of confronting and dealing with the issues that tore down the covenant in the first place."

Julie allowed David's words access to her heart. She heard some faint and shaming truth in them. With a sigh, she sat down and gathered her scattered, hurt feelings. She hugged her arms to her chest and stared at David for a long moment. Finally, she asked, her voice a cracking whisper, "What should I do?"

"The same thing I told Paul to do."

She gasped, sitting ramrod straight. "Paul's been here? He's already talked to you?"

"Paul's my sheep, too, Julie. And he's hurting, just like you." She had no comment, so David continued. "Go pray. Ask God to lead you. Then go sit down with Paul and talk it out. Honestly talk it out. Bare all your hurts and feelings. Get things out in the open, out in the light.

"I know that the camping trip is in jeopardy. As the minister of this church, I have to know where your commitments are. I have to know if you and Paul are going to run your separate lives, or if God is. Please find out. Sharon and I will be praying for you both."

Julie poured herself into prayer and when Paul called her at her office and asked her to meet for a quick lunch in a public place, she accepted, knowing that God would be with her. There remained an undercurrent of strain between her and Paul, a tension, a disquiet. She realized that this would not be a casual lunch between strained old friends. But a business lunch, heavy with decision making and standard-setting.

They met again at the Lincoln Memorial, in the fresh, bright air of a warm May morning. Neutral ground. Open, public, in plain view. The memorial was crowded this time, spilling over with tourists and school children, yet Julie saw Paul in the crowd instantly, in a gray business suit, leaning casually against a marble column. The sight of him caused her stomach to flutter. Why couldn't she separate herself from the peculiar magic he always seemed to work in her?

"Buy you a hot dog?" he asked, his guarded blue eyes searing through her as he took her arm at the bottom of the steps.

"Love one," she answered, forcing herself to smile, hoping she didn't gag on the food.

They found a Red Hot vendor parked on the grass at the side of the monument. Paul didn't have to ask how she liked her hot dog. He simply slathered mustard on one and mustard and relish on the second. He handed the latter to Julie. *Habits . . .* she thought. *Is there no forgetting?*

They walked slowly in the soft green grass, beside the reflecting pool, eating in silence, sipping cola from plastic straws between bites. In the distance, the sharp white tower of the Washington Monument poked into the crystalline blue sky, a obelisk that directed her eyes to the heavens.

"So," Paul said cautiously, carefully. "Where do I begin? How about with, 'I'm sorry.' " He shrugged. "I didn't mean for the other night to happen. I never meant to destroy the good thing God had revived between us." He stopped walking and turned and gazed down at her.

She felt her heart pounding, thumping. She swallowed. He continued, "The truth is, I wanted you. I wanted to make love to you again." A rueful smile flicked the corners of his mouth, softening the shield in his eyes. "After all, that aspect of our marriage was always so good." His words stirred mutual memories and in rapid fire succession, Julie recalled days and nights of love and tenderness. *Dangerous!* her mind warned. *We can't go back.*

She saw sincerity in his eyes. And compassion. "The other night . . . I led you down a path . . . I shouldn't have. . . ." His words came in slow, hesitant pauses. He was genuinely sorry, spiritually sorry, and she realized it.

Her own guard dropped and she met his gaze squarely. "It wasn't all your fault, Paul," she told him, bringing her own desires out into the open. "I wanted you, too." Her eyes did not waver and he tilted his head, surprised at the truth he saw in their depths. She held his look, feeling a release of the tightness in her chest.

"And what do you want now, Julie?"

This time, she could not answer him so honestly. She didn't know. "I think . . . I think I want to go back

129

to square one. Where we were before . . ." her words
trailed, ". . . before the other night."

The hooded cloud descended over his features again.
"Just a nice little friendship," he commented, not offering it as a question.

An uncomfortable flush crept up her neck. "Yes,"
she said, her voice a whisper. "No entanglements. No
involvements."

"Your will or God's?"

She wanted to bristle at his perception of her own
spiritual uncertainties, but she didn't. Involvement with
Paul . . . she didn't want to face that sort of soul-rending emotion again. She wasn't strong enough yet.

"And the camping trip?" he asked.

"Still on," she said. "I don't want to back out. Do
you?"

A grim line settled around his mouth. "No. I promised the kids."

"Then it's settled. We'll take the kids and things will
be like they were before between us."

He nodded briskly. "Yes. It's settled," he restated.
He lifted his arm and glanced at his watch. "I have to
be in court in an hour, come on. I'll walk you back to
your car."

She fell into step beside him, her heels clicking
against the concrete sidewalk. Things were settled, she
told herself. They'd put things back together. She was
safe and insulated and protected again from the storm
of those overwhelming emotions that hounded her like
banshees when Paul took her in his arms. Things were
settled. They were divorced. But they were still friends.
Wasn't that what God wanted?

Yet someplace, deep inside, she couldn't feel rest
and peace and satisfaction. "Things *are* settled," she
muttered inwardly.

*Julie wandered the empty streets for hours, numb
from the cold, more numb still from the memory of what
she'd seen. She felt dirty and used. It was Sunday morn-*

ing. *Nothing was open, except churches. But she didn't want to go there. She couldn't face people with tear-stained cheeks and red swollen eyes. She couldn't face God either. Why? Why had He let it happen? Why had He allowed it to happen? Her anguish came in fresh torrents.*

She still had her purse and some money. She took a cab to the airport. From there she caught a plane to Columbus. She'd go home. To her family. Yes! To her family. They would help her, comfort her. What would they say? Poor Julie! She grimaced at the thought of pity and condolences. She couldn't stand pity! What do you do when a marriage dies? Do you send flowers? Sympathy cards? How about a wake? Would anyone come?

Once home, Ruth Kreel held her daughter and let her cry out her grief. "You really should let Paul know that you're safe," she counseled.

Julie recoiled. Never! He could rot! "I don't want him near me ever again!" she erupted.

"He's your husband, Julie. Whatever he's done, he's still your husband."

Julie refused to believe what her mother was saying. She had expected sympathy. At least righteous indignation. "Not for long!" Julie spat through clenched teeth. "We're through!"

"Julie, you're not thinking rationally. Calm down," Ruth soothed.

Julie turned anguished eyes on her mother's face, too exhausted to think clearly. She needed to rest, to feel safe. "Please, let me stay, Mom. For a while. Until . . . until I get some things figured out."

"Honey!" Ruth cried, taking her daughter in her arms again. "Of course you can stay. We love you, Julie. We'll always stand by you. But sooner or later, you'll have to talk to Paul."

"Sooner" came two days later, when he arrived, unshaven, disheveled, drawn with worry and fear. She met him in her parents' old-fashioned parlor. The room was

filled with stiff Victorian chairs and a horse-hair sofa and antiques handed down from great-grandmother to granddaughter to daughter.

"My God, Julie!" his voice cracked with intensity and emotion. "I've been so worried. I didn't know where you'd gone! I had the police looking for you! Why did you run away?" His blue eyes roiled with the storm clouds of tortured emotions.

She backed away from the madman in front of her, shutting out his words, looking past his unkempt clothes. She saw him brushing rain from a woman's shoulders.

"Come home with me," he pleaded. "Please. We'll work it out."

"No," her word was final, cold. She couldn't feel. All sensation had gone. Even her fingertips were numb.

"Julie! You've got to listen! I was angry about your trip. I went to the party anyway. I had too much to drink. Bianca drove me home."

The look of hatred on her face stopped the flow of his words. "I hate you." The venom in her voice drove home her remark. "Get out of here. Go away from me. I don't want to ever see you again. Do you understand? Not ever."

Steel went over Paul's body. "You don't know what you're saying."

Her sardonic laugh punctuated the dead air in the parlor. "Spare me the lies!" she shouted. "You've been building to that night for a long time, Paul. Do you think I'm a fool? I've seen how you've looked at her! Watched how you've met with her!"

"That's not true!"

"Oh it's the truth, all right," she snapped, her anger flowing hot now, shame and humiliation washing over her. "You took her to bed in your mind long before you slept with her. You betrayed me. You betrayed our marriage. I will never forgive you. Now, get out! And don't you ever come into my life again!"

He watched her, measuring her, appraising her for a long moment. "What are you going to do, Julie?" His voice was dull, reasoning abandoned in the maelstrom of her anger.

She thirsted for vengeance, feeling its white-hot sword firmly in her grasp. "My lawyer will be in touch with you, Paul," she said, her voice driving hard the dagger of revenge. "You have a law degree. Figure it out."

"I don't want a divorce," he told her, offering resistance, yet sensing the end of the battle.

"And I never wanted to come home and find another woman in my bed!" she hissed, low and threatening. "Don't fight me, Paul. Don't you dare fight me!"

He raked his hand through his unruly hair. "What's to fight for, Julie? When you hate me so much."

Triumphantly, Julie backed off. She'd won. Paul would give her the divorce. But the taste of victory was not nearly so sweet as she thought it would be. It bothered her. But it didn't change her mind.

Preparations for the camping trip began in earnest. Meetings were held, agendas discussed. "Walk," Paul told the nine kids planning to take the trip. "If you walk now, you'll be in condition for the mountain trails. We'll be spending most of the time in a formal campsite. It has sites for our big tents plus showers, cooking pits, and some of life's nicer conveniences." He flashed Julie a grin, then continued.

"We'll spend one overnighter on the trail in a special shelter with shelves for bunks, so you'll have to backpack bedrolls, cooking gear, and a change of clothes as well as blankets, a small ice chest and food. This stuff will get heavy real quick if you're not in top form," he warned. "The last day before we head home, we'll take the canoe trip down the river. Play some tennis and strengthen those rowing arms," he grinned.

He passed out lists of what clothes to pack, lists of supplies each would be responsible for bringing. He insisted on signed medical releases and parental permission slips. Very thorough, Julie thought. But then Paul was always very thorough.

Since many of the kids had gone on a prior camping trip with the church, they had much of the equipment and were familiar with much of the routine. Julie had not, so she walked every evening after work, following his instructions, vowing to be ready for the adventure, to be able to do her share and not be dependent on Paul for anything. Yet it was Paul who took her to the sporting goods store one Saturday to buy the essentials of sleeping bag, hiking shoes, backpack—the many required items she didn't own.

Julie insisted Cindy and Rob go with them. "More fun," she told him.

"More safe," he countered knowingly.

The store, specializing in camping and survivalist paraphernalia, caused her to gasp. So many products! "It's an industry!" she said, surveying aisle after aisle of merchandise—tents, clothing, food, cooking utensils. "People buy all this stuff? *That* many people camp?" she asked, wide-eyed.

"You bet," Paul confirmed. "First, hiking boots," he continued, all-business, taking her hand to the corner of the complex that featured footwear. "Comfortable, durable, heavy . . . in case of snakebite," he said, picking up shoes and scanning them to meet his criteria.

"Snakebite?" Julie asked, a flutter in her stomach.

He flashed her a lopsided grin. "Unless you bite one first."

"Funny," she told him, but settled on the pair of boots he recommended.

They passed from section to section, choosing the things she would need. "Ugh!" Cindy said, wrinkling her nose. "Why do sleeping bags come in such dull colors?"

Paul unfurled one on the floor and said, "This will do. Big enough for two," he commented lazily, ignoring Julie's warning look. She gritted her teeth. Paul was intent on tormenting and teasing her. She told herself that she wouldn't rise to the bait.

134

They finally moved to the food section of the giant store. Again, Julie gaped at the array and variety of items available for camping enthusiasts. Dehydrated, freeze-dried, pounded, packaged, reconstituted—her head spun at the selection of food.

"Water purification tablets," Paul said, throwing packets into their shopping cart.

"What? I thought there was running water at the campsite?" she asked.

"Good water at the campsite. But not on the trail."

"Hey, Cindy!" Rob taunted. "No washing your hair every three hours."

Cindy stuck her tongue out at her brother. "You may bathe every day at the campsite," Paul assured them, "but not on the overnighter. Bring plenty of deodorant, Germaine," Paul poked at Rob with a good-natured smile.

"Beef stroganoff?" Julie asked, incredulous at the exotic sampling of foodstuffs. She fingered the foil-wrapped pouches. "Chicken stew? Carrots? Corn? Rice pudding?" She shook her head and watched Paul toss in handfuls of the dehydrated offerings.

"You didn't think we were going to live off bear meat, did you?"

"Don't be a turkey!" Julie snapped, embarrassed at her own naïveté and lack of experience.

With her words, a shared memory flared between them. A memory so potent that Paul turned and fixed her with a riveting stare. A memory so powerful that Julie spontaneously clamped her hand across her mouth like a child who'd accidently spilled the beans. Their eyes locked, and Julie felt color, hot, scarlet color burn up her neck and across her cheeks.

"What's with you two?" Cindy asked, bewildered, her eyes jumping between them as if it were a tennis match. When neither offered her an explanation, Cindy shrugged, annoyed, at missing the unspoken thing they shared. "Weird!" she said in total exasperation and stamped her foot peevishly.

135

Julie was the first to break eye contact. "Let's get this over with," she said stiffly. "We haven't got all day, you know." She pushed the cart forward, gripping the handle for dear life, trying to erase the memory from her mind, and gather herself into the present, to forget one very vivid Thanksgiving Day and the taste of Paul on her hungering, eager mouth.

Asunder. Julie understood exactly what it meant to be put asunder. To be divided . . . ripped apart . . . hacked, shredded, torn. Asunder was an event, a happening, a breaking and a cauterizing. You tore apart a whole thing into two halves. Two fleshes. Marriage . . . one flesh. Asunder . . . two fleshes. End of cycle.

"I just wish you wouldn't act so hastily," Ruth told her daughter as they sat together in Julie's childhood bedroom.

"My mind's made up, Mom," Julie said tersely. "The papers are in the works. The divorce is going to happen." Her mother's attitude, her defense of a marriage so easily sold out, annoyed Julie tremendously. "Who's side are you on, anyway?" Julie snapped with more anger than she had intended.

Ruth shook her gray-streaked head and leveled her brown eyes at Julie. "I don't take sides. But Julie, this is a marriage we're talking about. Not a high school break-up."

Unable to sit any longer on the bed, Julie began pacing the room like a caged tiger. "Marriage!" The very word left a bad taste in her mouth.

"Paul's called and called you," Ruth reminded her. "Won't you at least sit down and talk to him? I know both of you could sit down with Pastor Dunsmore and talk this thing out. . . ."

"No!" Julie exploded. Pastor Dunsmore! She couldn't imagine revealing her most intimate thoughts and feelings to the benign white-haired man who'd been her minister all her young life.

She stopped her restless roaming in front of her oak

trimmed bookcase, opened the glass door, and extracted an old book, randomly, to keep her hands busy. Mother Goose, the title read. How simple life used to be! she thought. How simple and uncluttered. She read silently,

"Peter, Peter pumpkin eater. . . . Had a wife and couldn't keep her. . . ."

Her head throbbed.

"Mom," Julie turned to gaze into her mother's care-lined face. "I understand how you and Dad feel about divorce. I used to feel the same way." Her voice trailed, then resumed on a stronger note. "But circumstances change things. People change. So do their feelings. I'm getting the divorce and that's final."

Familiar rhymes whirled in front of her on the yellowed pages.

"Oh dear, what can the matter be? Johnny's so long at the fair. . . ."

Her eyes burned.

She paused, decided to reveal everything and plunged ahead. "I've sent off some resumés to ad agencies in other cities. I'll be moving just as soon as I can land a good job."

"You don't have to leave, Julie."

"Yes, I do," Julie said with determination. "I have to start over. Preferably someplace far away from all these old memories. I can't go back to New York. I don't want to stay here in Columbus. I'm a good copywriter and my old agency will give me a strong letter of recommendation. I want to work. I—I need to work." Again, her voice trailed and she resumed the random, purposeless thumbing through the old book of nursery verses.

"Humpty Dumpty sat on a wall. . . . Humpty Dumpty had a great fall. . . . All the king's horses. . . . All the king's men. . . ."

The words began to blur before her eyes. Tears threatened. She sucked in fiercely. "I understand how old Humpty felt," she said distractedly, inundated by a vast, sweeping despair.

Ruth caught her gaze and held it with her own. "Maybe he asked the wrong King."

Julie slammed the book shut. Three months later, responding to a job offer, she moved to Washington.

CHAPTER 10

THE CHURCH PARKING LOT hosted the swarm of vehicles in the pre-dawn hours like ants at a picnic site. Sleepy-eyed parents and kids converged to the point where the church van sat waiting to receive its passengers for the trip into the mountains. Paul locked the metal cover over the trailer hooked to the back of the van that contained the gear, backpacks, and equipment, and signaled for the nine high school kids to climb inside the van's roomy interior.

Julie followed, sluggishly, shaking off the restless night she'd spent in bed in anticipation for the week-long camping trip. Tess hung next to her, watching Rob and Cindy board with Jud, Tina, Carmen, Joan, Mike, Steve, and Terry. "You ready for this?" Tess asked skeptically into Julie's ear.

"Prepared, yes," Julie told her. "Ready, no. I don't think I'll ever be ready."

It was Tess who commented, "Seven days in the wilds with Paul. You going to be all right?"

"Seven days, well chaperoned," she countered. "Yes. I'll be fine. But thanks for asking."

"Have fun." Tess squeezed her hand in farewell.

"And don't worry about Hector! I'll take good care of him."

Julie climbed into the front bucket seat of the van and crossed her arms against the early morning chill. Even though it was June, the morning air still had a bite to it. Paul scooted behind the wheel and she kept her eyes front, trying hard to ignore the fresh tangy smell of his aftershave and his bright parting comments to the parents. He was a little too bright and cheerful for Julie to face this morning.

David Wilson leaned in the window. "Where's that famous Kreel smile?"

"Ask me after I've spent two days in the wilderness," she offered him a hint of her usually dimpled smile.

"You'll be fine," Paul interjected.

It isn't the camping trip that's unnerving me, she thought. *It's the seven days of constant contact with you!* But she couldn't say that, of course.

"Beware of bears and snakes," David whispered loudly, causing two of the girls to squeal and giggle.

"It's not the bears and snakes that bother campers this time of the year," Paul said. "It's the wolves," he deadpanned.

David chuckled, Rob guffawed, and Julie shot Paul a scowl and hunkered down into the seat, tugging the collar of her wind breaker closer around her throat in a gesture of dismissal. With a lurch, the van pulled out of the parking lot.

The city fell away in the light morning traffic and soon the van turned onto Route 50, heading west, away from the breaking rays of the sun, chasing the steady gray gloom of the receding night until the clouds eventually dispersed it with the brilliant light of the climbing sun. The trees thickened along the sides of the road, verdant and splendid in the warming new day.

Julie quickly lay aside her foreboding as she led songs, harmonizing with Paul's voice automatically. By mid-morning everyone was warm and relaxed, Paul's

140

infectious charm acting as a glue for all of them. Even Julie smiled brightly, beginning to anticipate with eagerness their arrival at the wilderness camping site.

The route dipped south and the scenery changed again, as the road wound higher and higher into the foothills and up into the mountains. Breathlessly, Julie watched the peaks hover in the distance, purple and hazy, noble and time worn. Overhanging granite walls hugged the side of the road. She wondered what it must have been like to forge the road through the unyielding earth.

The kids quieted, some dozing in the gathering warmth. Julie poured steaming cups of coffee from a thermos bottle for Paul as she sipped some from a styrofoam cup to keep her stomach from snarling about her missed breakfast. Mentally, she inventoried her personal belongings. T-shirts, jacket, sweatshirt, three pairs of jeans, shorts, tennis shoes, thongs, underclothes, and six changes of socks. She remembered what Paul had told her. "Wear two pair of socks for hiking, one over the other. You get better padding, plus your outer pair becomes your dry pair for sleeping at night."

It was the lightest she had ever packed for traveling, but the trail seemed no place for glamour. *Dummy!* she chided silently. *Glamour for what?* Julie turned her thoughts to the kids in the back and turned slightly to see her charges. Cindy sat glumly, withdrawn and preoccupied, certainly not her usual bubbly self. Jud also had retreated to the exclusive fellowship of Rob and Steve. Problems already. Great! Julie sighed. That's all they needed.

She reminded herself that the trip was also an opportunity for spiritual renewal—for *all* of them. She hoped that Jud and Cindy's tiff didn't dampen the trip for everybody. Julie decided that she'd speak to Cindy in private if things didn't improve by the end of the day.

Paul stopped the van for lunch at a roadside picnic

area cut from the side of a mountain. It was large enough for only two picnic tables and a shelter with a sheer, fifty foot drop of rocks and grass down its far side. They sat munching prepackaged sandwiches, chips, and sodas, making small talk with one another. Julie noted that the situation with Cindy and Jud did not improve, but at least Rob seemed to be having a good time.

It was late afternoon when they rolled into the camp-site and Julie was pleasantly surprised by the clean, civilized, comfortable look of it. "It has a store!" She pointed in utter amazement at a small convenience store at the entrance of the campground.

"Well, you didn't think I could live on dehydrated turkey for seven days," Paul quipped, giving her a sly wink.

She ignored his remark and watched the bathhouses pass as the van wove slowly around the parameters of the grounds. Paul found their assigned tent sites and parked. The kids fairly shot off the van and began to unpack the trailer, most already familiar with the du-ties of setting up camp.

Julie watched, feeling inadept and useless. As usual, she found herself glancing covertly at Paul, fascinated, yet irritated over the undeniable attraction he held for her. *Why can't he be ugly?* she thought sourly.

They assembled large tents over the pre-cleared, earth packed ground so that campers could sleep com-fortable and unaccosted by roaming wildlife. The girls' tent went up first. Julie crawled inside the airy nylon structure once it was lashed and secured discovering it surprisingly roomy. With the pads and bedrolls spread out she had the illusion of being tucked inside the tent of some fabled desert sheik.

The boys' tent was pitched and soon everyone broke for a walk around the neat, picturesque grounds. The lull brought Paul to Julie's side as she sat beneath a large shade tree fanning her face with a paper napkin.

"What's with Cindy?" he asked, lowering himself next to her.

"You've noticed, too." She mopped perspiration then balled up the napkin into a tight wad.

"Cindy wears her heart on her sleeve. Who hasn't noticed?"

He was right. Cindy couldn't hide her feelings, good or bad. Maybe that's why Julie felt such a kinship for the girl. She reminded her so much of herself at that age. She'd worn her heart on her sleeve then also.

"I'll speak to her if she doesn't perk up," Julie told him, turning her mind from the past.

"I'd appreciate it," he said, letting his eyes rest on the curve of her neck.

She moved away, anxious not to meet his gaze, afraid of letting him get too near her, uneasy with her own responses to him.

Their respite was short-lived as the kids came trooping back, ravenous and clamoring for supper. The boys built a fire in the brick fire shell and soon Julie had the girls preparing the dinner. Because of the convenience store, they bought fresh meat, wrapping hamburger patties and corn in foil and letting the packets roast in the coals.

They feasted as shadows lengthened and afterward watched the sun disappear over a distant mountain ridge while the stars slowly came out, salting the dark sky with flecks of light. Cindy's mood improved, so Julie decided against confronting her, but it was obvious that there was a current of unrest between her and Jud.

Someone brought out the makings for "s'mores"—graham cracker, chocolate, and marshmallow treats—and they toasted them over the dying embers of the fire. Finally, Paul read Scripture, prayed a prayer of thanks and protection, and suggested that everybody go to bed. "The morning comes early," he said. "And we'll begin a long hike immediately after breakfast."

Julie and the girls drifted off to the showers. The

water was warm, the soap fragrant. Julie reveled under the refreshing spray. Like a wicked muse, the drumming water reminded her of the times she and Paul had showered together. Her skin flushed hotly, and with an angry twist she shut off the shower spray, dried, dressed, and padded hastily back to the airy tent. She climbed inside and settled under the folds of her sleeping bag.

The voices of the girls droned on around her for several minutes, reminding her of teenage slumber parties. Julie snuggled into the cocoon warmth of the bag, trying hard to drive off the persistent, nagging memories that flitted around her mind like pesky mosquitoes. Gratefully, sleep reached out for her and her last conscious thought was the line from Genesis, "And the evening and the morning were the first day."

The first gray streaks of light across the sky caused Julie to awaken. At first, she felt disoriented and lost. But the overhead arch of the tent caused her mind to sharpen. She gathered her thoughts like wandering chicks, pulling them inside her one by one. Everyone else still slept. Noiselessly, Julie slipped out of her warm bag, shivering as she tugged on jeans and a sweatshirt. She collected her soap, toothbrush, and make-up pouch and left for the bathhouse. Refreshed, she returned, dug out her Bible and went into the woods to read and pray.

The morning began to stir, painting red and gold streaks overhead. The smell of the woods blanketed her as she crunched through the cool green foliage looking for a place to settle in to read. She found an old stump and sat down. She filled her lungs with the freshness of the morning, delighting in the chirping of the birds and the smell of earth and dampness. How beautiful God's world was! She read, prayed, rejoiced, and gloried in the new day.

Consider the lilies of the field, They toil not, Neither do they spin. Yet I tell you that Solomon and all his glory was not arrayed as one of these.

She found the words beautiful and comforting.

Look at the birds of the air, that they do not sow, neither do they reap, and yet your heavenly Father feeds them. Are you not worth much more than they?

It was true. God had always cared for her, her physical needs, her emotional needs. Even in her darkest times, He had been with her. A sense of peace fell on Julie and she saw something as she had not seen it before. Paul—and all that had happened between them—was part of God's purpose for her life. The revelation was stunning. Why had she not realized that before? Why had she only seen Paul as a mistake of her choosing instead of a tool for God's plan for her life? What had they gained together? A broken marriage? Yes, but a lot of love, too. God had given her to Paul and Paul to her. Their love—bold and physical, soft and dependent—had been a gift.

She had never loved anyone before Paul. She had never loved anyone since him. Why? Was it because Paul was still part of God's plan for her life? Julie sucked in her breath, opening her eyes wide, staring into space but not seeing the trees or ground or sky. She saw instead into the dark well of her own hurt. Hesitantly, she poked into the murky waters of memory. Pain met her, but so did soothing.

She had loved Paul wildly, recklessly, totally. She had felt betrayed by him. So betrayed, so hurt, so abused that she had never wanted him near her again. Why? To protect herself from the hurt? But if God was protecting her and watching over her, then why did she need to do it? Julie had no answer. Somewhere, along the torturous path of her past, Julie had stopped leaning on God for support and had begun to lean on herself. She realized it now with blinding clarity. And the realization left her dazed and finally convicted.

What was it Paul had said to her that September day in the conference room? "When God met me, I felt such peace." She had not felt peace since the day she swore to divorce him. Yet divorce wasn't wrong. It wasn't evil. God allowed it. "Because of your hardness of heart," David had told her.

Julie turned to Mark 10 in her Bible and reread the passages about divorce. She'd always thought of them as justification for divorcing Paul. But now she saw them in a new light. She and Paul had been one flesh. Could it be possible that they were still one flesh? Still joined by the circle of covenant despite the divorce? Julie shook her head in an effort to clear it. So many questions! So many feelings and revelations!

The day had grown steadily brighter around her. The sounds from the camp came through her senses slowly, but persistently. She had to go back. They would be looking for her. Reluctantly, Julie closed her Bible. God had revealed much to her this morning. She had much to think about, pray about. She released herself to His will in the warming of the new day, sorrowful over her stubbornness and lack of insight about her life and God's leading. Julie felt her spirits lift with the rising of the day. She hurried back to the campsite, eager to be pliable clay in the Potter's masterful hands.

"I was beginning to think you'd run away," Paul said. His tone was half-teasing, but there was an undercurrent of worry and tenseness.

She flashed him a brilliant smile. "I'm sorry. I was reading and forgot about the time."

She saw his eyes graze her face, study it, seeing things he couldn't name. She wanted to share something with him. Something personal that would have meaning only for him. She held his eyes and said, "I won't run away again, Paul. Not ever. Please believe that."

He tipped his head, grasping to hold onto the elusive

message she was sending. She wanted to say more, but a wail from Cindy snapped their heads around. "There's a spider in my shoe! Help!"

Paul sighed and headed over to protect the trembling girl from the reality of life in the wilderness. Julie carefully covered over the intensity of her newfound peace and understanding to begin a new day.

Paul kept his distance from Julie. She needed the time alone, without the interference of her confused feelings for him. She had many things to take to God before she could talk to Paul. And the activity of the camping trip provided them both with proximity but not with intimacy. They were busy, focused, together, yet apart.

The days brought all of them closer together. The group studied Scripture, hiked, ate, slept, prayed, prepared for the night on the trail. All too soon, Julie felt time slipping away from her. But she refused to do anything in haste. This time she wanted God in the driver's seat, guiding, leading, carrying her into His purposes. He led. Julie vowed to follow.

The only dark spot on the experience was the strain between Cindy and Jud. The tension between them had not eased. And it wasn't until they were on the trail, hiking, headed for the sleeping shelter at the crest of the mountain path that Julie was able to confront Cindy about it.

"Okay, Cindy," Julie said, striding along beside the dark-haired teen on the narrow trail, "tell me what's happening with you and Jud." It was not a request. Cindy began talking slowly, between breaths as they worked their way up the twisting trail, their backpacks heavy in the thinning air.

"He—he wants to date other girls. He—he says he likes me and all, but that we should both date others."

The situation became clear to Julie immediately. "And you don't."

Cindy turned sad green eyes toward Julie. "I love

147

him, Julie." They trudged on, stepping single file through a very narrow pass. When Julie walked beside Cindy again, the girl said hotly, "You don't believe me, do you? You think a 15 year old doesn't know anything about 'love.' " She said the word mockingly.

"That's not true. I think you are in love with Jud."

"You do?" Cindy gasped, stopping dead on the trail. Julie nudged her along so that Carmen wouldn't run into their backs.

"Yes." Julie remembered vividly those first stirrings of unabashed love that she had felt for Paul. She hadn't been fifteen, but the feelings had been the same. Bittersweet. Agony and ecstasy. "But moping around, clinging to him like a vine, smothering him with guilt, and trying to elicit his pity isn't any way to hold him."

Cindy stopped dead and blinked at Julie. "That's—that's not true!"

"Isn't it?" Julie continued. She hated to hurt Cindy, but someone had to tell her the truth. "Has it worked so far?" she asked. "Has Jud stopped wanting to date other girls? Is he staying with you out of a sense of obligation?"

Cindy's cheeks flushed scarlet. She tried to sputter a rebuttal. Julie reached out and took her arm, gently, softening her voice. "Is that what you want? To keep him at all costs? To maybe have him start disliking you because you're strangling him with your 'love?' "

Luminous tears sparkled in Cindy's eyes. Julie's heart went out to her, but she steeled herself, knowing that sometimes the truth hurt, but it didn't make it less the truth. "No," Cindy said miserably.

"Then let him go," Julie told her kindly.

"But what if I lose him?"

"Love takes risks, Cindy. 'It's kind, not jealous, not arrogant.' " Julie quoted the familiar words from Corinthians 13 for Cindy, ". . . *and it doesn't take into account a wrong suffered!*" The impact of those words hitting her memory almost took Julie's breath.

... it bears all things, believes all things, hopes all things, endures all things.

Julie blinked, suddenly dumb-struck by the glaring light of revelation from those words.

The truth came to her with such clarity, with such force that her knees went weak and her hands trembled. It wasn't that she had loved Paul too much. It was that she hadn't loved him nearly enough!

"Julie? Julie? Are you all right?" Cindy's anxious voice penetrated through Julie's consciousness. "You look so pale. Do you feel all right?"

Julie blinked at the teen's frightened face. "I'll call Mr. Shannon," Cindy started.

"No!" Julie reached out a restraining hand and shook her head to clear it, to bring herself back into the present. "No, really, honey. I—I'm fine. I just felt a little sick to my stomach. Probably those dehydrated eggs we had for breakfast," she offered lamely, making a face at the same time.

"If you're sure," Cindy said skeptically.

Julie put her arm around the young girl's shoulder and squeezed. "Think about what I told you. Please."

Cindy nodded, scuffing the rocky ground with the toe of her boot. "I will."

Julie smiled, feeling burdens, cares, and problems falling off of her like scales. God had showed Julie herself. And while the portrait wasn't exactly pretty, it was real. She thanked Him for that silently, still awed by the impact of His newest revelation.

"We'd better hurry," she told Cindy, tugging her along the trail to catch up with the hikers who'd already passed them. "Suddenly, I'm starving! And it's almost time for lunch. How do you feel about reconstituted ham salad?" She allowed her laugh to flow, free and light and golden in the crisp mountain air.

The shelter at the top of the trail was a three-sided, split log building with a brick fire pit and stacked rows of planks lining the walls, wide enough to hold a bed-roll. It resembled a haphazard bunkhouse, but it was dry and would keep the wind out. After supper, exhaustion swept over Julie as she watched the boys in charge of K.P. sponge off the utensils from fire-heated water in a bucket; water they'd carried with them in gallon jugs for drinking and washing. She listened to the low buzz of conversation between the kids, remembering the security and safety of the campsite at the foot of the mountain below.

The campsite! Suddenly, it seemed like a resort to Julie by comparison to the rustic shelter surrounding them. She longed to take a warm shower and wash off the grime of the trail. *Tomorrow* she told herself. *Tomorrow I'll soak until I'm wrinkled.*

Someone made a halfhearted attempt to sing after Paul read the Scriptures, but the effort proved too much and soon the group had dozed off one by one, tucked neatly away on their wooden shelves. All except for Julie. As tired as she was, sleep would not come for her. The strange sounds of the night, the rustling of the wind in the trees, the darkness . . . all made her restless and jittery.

Finally, she got up, tugged her jacket over her sweatshirt, slid her tennis shoes over her heavy socks and stepped out of the protective covering of the shelter. It was surprisingly cold. She shivered and hugged her chest, walking a short distance to keep from waking anyone with her night wanderings.

The trees shot like dark arrows into a dark sky. A sliver of a moon shone above and she gazed at it reflectively until the sound of someone whispering her name caused her to gasp and whirl.

"I didn't mean to scare you," Paul stepped beside her from the trees. "I saw you wander off and I wondered if you were all right."

His body next to hers filled her with comfort and somehow the night didn't seem so forlorn and lonely. "Yes, I—I just couldn't sleep."

"Come on," he urged taking her hand. "Let's walk."

His hand felt warm as it enveloped hers. They strolled for a few minutes in silence under the whispering trees and the scrutiny of the moon. "It certainly is dark," Julie commented once they were away from the shelter.

A warm chuckle started in Paul's throat. "That's why they call it night."

"Whose idea was this camping trip anyway?" she asked, catching the mood of his teasing.

"You love it. Besides, you've turned into a real pro. Now you'll be all set for next year."

She groaned but was inwardly pleased that he had complimented her wilderness efforts. They stood comfortably for a few minutes while the night settled in, chilly and sharp all around them. "I talked to Cindy today," Julie said, breaking the silence. "She and Jud are breaking up."

"I figured as much," Paul's voice came from behind her. He rested his hands on her shoulders. Her neck muscles knotted with tension. "You're tight as a spring."

"Mules were created for backpacking," she quipped. "Not 98-pound weaklings."

Paul's easy laugh sounded in her ear and he began massaging the tight, sore muscles. It felt wonderful! But as his fingers relieved one kind of tension, they incited another kind. She wanted to turn and face him. She wanted to have him hold her; to feel a sense of oneness and unity with him; to be a part of him, an extension of him.

"Julie," his voice was low. His body blocked the cool breeze from her back, sending the familiar warmth of his form up her length. He rested his chin on the top of her head. "Julie, I've been waiting for some time alone with you." Her heart hammered.

"I want to tell you something. I talked to Don Freytag right before we left." She said nothing, poised between feeling and action. "He thinks that he and Mary will be able to take over the youth group at the end of this month since activities are pretty light during the summer."

"They want their job back?" she asked, a warning bell clanging against the warmth of her contentment.

"Yes. And as soon as they take it back, I'll be leaving Washington."

CHAPTER 11

"LEAVING?" SHE ALMOST GAGGED on the word. "But where will you go? What will you do?"

Paul draped his arm casually across her shoulders and she turned to look up at him. The pale glimmer of the moon was too weak to bathe his face in light, but she knew the set of his features by heart. She knew the look his eyes held. She knew the full curve of pensiveness his mouth had assumed.

"I'm not sure where yet. But I'm very sure about what I want to do." His voice took on an edge of excitement as he shared his career vision with her. "I want to set up my own law practice. But I want to counsel and advise Christians. I want to help them understand God's standards and principles and I want to help them apply God's ways to their lives.

"I want to do litigation for them; but only as it upholds the Bible. I want to help Christians work out their differences with other Christians as well as to help Christians fighting against the world." The fervor in his voice mounted. "Did you know, Julie, that at the start of this country's history, no man could be a lawyer unless he first had a divinity degree?

"How far we've come," Paul mused. "Today, we live in a 'no-fault' world. No-fault divorce, no-fault car accidents, no-fault murder. But, Julie, God holds man accountable. We are responsible for what we do here on earth. We are bound by His law whether we want to believe it or not. I think I can build the kind of practice that will help men understand their accountability."

His voice had dropped, until all Julie heard was the winsome sound of the wind in the trees. "I—I think you can, too, Paul," she told him. "There's a real need for righteousness in our judicial system." She let her words dwindle, knowing they were true, yet hollow. Paul was leaving. Wasn't that what she had wanted all along? Wasn't that what she'd prayed for since last September? *Why do I feel so empty?*

"As to where I'll go, well, I'm not sure," he continued. "Maybe to the Midwest."

"You'd have to take the bar exams again," she offered. *Looking for an excuse to make him stay?* some wicked imp whispered to her conscience. Hatefully, she shoved the idea aside and shrugged. "No matter. Wherever you hang out your shingle, I know you'll be a success."

"Success," he mused. "How different success looks to me now. A really successful man is one who has his priorities in order. A man with God at his center—not himself." His words impacted her. There was a time when Paul would have never uttered those words, much less practiced them. But now he would build his dreams alone, without her. Their separate courses were set.

"Think you can sleep now?" His words broke through her veil of melancholy.

"Yes," she admitted. "Yes, suddenly I'm very tired."

He took her hand and walked her slowly back to the shelter. "You're cold."

"It'll pass once I snuggle into that sleeping bag," she countered, trying to keep her tone light. "You helped me pick a good one. It's very warm." *Sleeping bags!* Her life was changing all over once again, and all she could prattle on about was a sleeping bag!

"Good night," Paul said as she slipped away from him. Julie struggled into the bag, fending off the chilling night air. But since it was more than the night that made her cold, it took longer than usual for her to capture warmth.

The morning on the trail broke clear and cold. Paul led the shivering group to a small clearing where they sat and listened to the words of the Psalms. Paul's rich, resonant voice rang in the cold, biting air, filling Julie with a sense of wonder at the majesty and beauty of God's world. She looked from face to face among the kids, realizing that they, too, had been touched by the grandeur of the creation around them.

The pungent smell of resins blended with the dark, loamy aroma of fresh-turned earth. She filled her lungs, drinking it in like an addicting draught. Green, abundant moss and wildflowers in riotous hues of red and orange and yellow and purple carpeted the ground. Suddenly, Julie felt revitalized, refreshed, and buoyant. She stored away the conversation of the previous night, rededicating herself to be attuned to God's will. If Paul was leaving, then she had to be sensitive to what God now wanted for her life.

Later, they feasted on a breakfast of pancakes, warm honey, and dried beef jerky. They washed it down with water, cleaned up, and policed the site for trash and started back down the trail, an easier feat than going up had been. They arrived at the campsite by midafternoon where Julie took her long-promised shower.

The next morning, they broke camp, packed the tents and gear in the trailer, and headed for the river and the canoe trip.

"This is the most fun of all!" Cindy bubbled from the back seat of the van as they drove to the canoe rental area.

Julie was glad that the girl had regained some of her

former good spirits. Even though she and Jud had not worked out their differences, Cindy had seemed to come to terms with reality and was acting more like her former, happy-go-lucky self. It helped everyone's mood.

"Here's the plan," Paul told them as he maneuvered the van toward the rental station. "We'll get the canoes, paddle down river, have lunch near the rapids, and maybe," he paused, "*maybe* if they're not too treacherous we'll paddle through them instead of carrying the canoes around them."

Applause and cheers broke out. Julie felt a moment of trepidation, then banished it. Paul continued. "In the meantime, one of the rangers from the canoe area will drive the van for us to the disembarkment site. I figure we'll get there by midafternoon, pick-up the van, and then head home."

Everybody groaned their displeasure at having to end the outing. Julie felt an acute letdown. It had been fun. Natural and fun and renewing. She and Paul had been a real team. Julie halted the direction her thoughts had taken. The team was about to be broken up—forever.

At the rental site, a ranger explained the rules and procedures to them. He issued life jackets to everyone and a walkie-talkie to Paul. "There's a lot of wilderness between here and the finish," the big-boned, red-headed man told them. "Don't drop the thing in the river!" he warned with a good-natured laugh.

The water appeared calm and sluggish as Julie climbed into the canoe, the morning warm, promising to grow hotter as the day lengthened. She had dressed in a T-shirt, shorts, and tennis shoes at Paul's direction, "You'll get drenched if we go through the rapids, but you'll dry quickly in the heat."

They rented four canoes, dispersing the stronger rowers among the weaker ones. Each canoe carried some supplies wrapped in featherweight waterproof coverings. Backpacks with a change of clothes and personal items were stashed under seats. Julie gingerly settled onto the center seat of the tipsy canoe. She wondered at how the American Indians had ever managed to travel in the things. Cindy sat in front of her, Steve behind. Paul took Joan and Carmen with him and the remainder of the kids divided up with Rob and Jud heading up separate canoes.

Cindy cast an envious glance at her blond, green-eyed friend Tina who sat snugly in a canoe with Jud, but Julie started a stream of chatter to distract the glum-faced teen. Soon Cindy resumed her cheerful manner.

Their paddles knifed through the water and the line of canoes snaked through the bends and curves of the river effortlessly. "I guess the Indians knew what they were doing after all," she mumbled and Cindy asked, "Huh?"

Trees drooped lazily over the banks of the river. In places the banks gave way to rocks and rose steep and jagged from the edge of the water. As the sun rose higher and higher, Julie's arms and shoulders began to ache with the repetition of the paddle movement. The life jacket began to chafe slightly under the movement of her arms and her stomach began to growl for lunch.

As if reading her mind, Paul called over from his canoe, "Listen closely and you'll hear the roar of the rapids. We'll go ashore and eat in about a half-hour!"

Julie listened. From far away she heard the rush of water surging over rocks. It sounded like a constant drum roll, reverberating with the swish from a snare drum. "Think we'll paddle over them?"

Paul flashed her a smile, his muscles reaching fluidly to draw back the paddle. "The ranger said the water was high. That means less danger of hitting rocks."

"That makes my day!" Julie called back to him drily.

He tossed his head backward and laughed. She watched the sun glance off his dark curls and his eyes turn deep, dark blue in the glaring light. "High water means fast water!" he shouted. "It'll be like shooting through a water flume."

Rob sent up an eager cheer. "Let's go for it!" he urged.

Soon, the sound of the rapids filled the air. Paul signaled for everyone to hit the shore and once they had landed and secured the canoes, they walked around the bend and stared at the plummeting, foaming rapids. Julie blinked in disbelief.

"Paddle through those!" she gasped. "You must be kidding!"

Paul chuckled and tapped her nose with his forefinger. "Of course, you less hearty ones can carry your canoes around. We'll meet up with you downstream."

Her ire rose. If he could do it, so could she! "Maybe after a little lunch," she said glancing at Carmen and Steve who gave her a thumbs up sign.

They set up a small camp, in the woods, away from the rush of the river. Peacefully, the green broad leaves of oaks and ash and maple sheltered them from the noonday sun. Julie flexed her sore arms and lazily munched on an apple while the group languished under the trees, collecting their strength, gathering their reserves for the run down the rapids. Paul had taken a walk with Rob, and Julie felt herself missing his presence. "Get used to it!" she said under her breath.

"Julie," Cindy came up next to her, scraping the toe of her pink tennis shoe over the ground, "can we talk?"

Julie smiled warmly, chasing off her lethargy. "Sure. Want to walk, too?"

Cindy nodded and the two of them moved off into the sun-flecked greenery of the Virginia woods. Julie plucked a leaf and pondered the intricate network of veins along its surface, giving Cindy time to gather her thoughts.

"I—I just want to thank you for what you said the other day," she began, her voice soft and subdued. "You're right. I can't make Jud care about me again."

Julie looked at the girl tenderly, absorbing her inner

anguish. Cindy's bouncy black hair caught the sunlight. Her pretty heart-shaped face puckered in painful concentration. "I—I've been praying about it. As—as soon as I get home, I'm going to have a long talk with him. It's best if we both start dating others again." Her voice trailed off into a small sound of misery.

Julie swallowed. How could she comfort her? How could she tell Cindy she understood how much she was hurting? The woods broke in front of them into a circular clearing. A couple, standing in the open, did not see them approach. A tall muscular boy held a girl's hand. They were deep in intimate conversation.

Julie and Cindy's eyes flitted from boy to girl in dawning surprise. A brown-haired boy with brown eyes. Jud. A light-haired girl with green eyes. Tina. A strangled cry escaped from Cindy's disbelieving throat and everyone stood briefly staring at each other. Shocked. Stunned. Stupefied.

Cindy turned and bolted. "Cindy! Wait! Honey . . . please . . . wait!" Julie cried, breaking into a run. Jud fell in next to her matching her stride for stride, each chasing the fleeing figure.

"Julie!" he struggled. "I—I'm sorry! I didn't mean for for her to see. . . ."

Hotly, Julie snapped, "Save it, Jud! Just catch her!"

They burst into the camp area amid bewildered looks from the rest of the group. Cindy first, hurtling blindly toward the river bank. Julie, gritting her teeth and gasping. Jud, detouring around a rock and falling behind. Paul and Rob straightened, startled from their conversation beside a tree.

"What the . . . ?" Paul asked.

"Stop her!" Julie cried.

But Cindy had reached one of the canoes. In blind panic, she shoved it into the water, leaped in, and wildly dipped the paddle, desperately striving to force the canoe forward, away from the shoreline.

"Don't!" Paul shouted. "Cindy! No! The rapids!"

But she didn't stop. Instead the canoe bobbed forward, righting itself beneath Cindy's weight and then caught in the swift current of the river. Helplessly, Julie saw the canoe surge forward, like a shot arrow, skimming pointlessly over the surging, foaming water toward the rapids. The boat smashed against an underwater rock, tipped and spun wildly, like a cork caught in a whirlpool. Cindy screamed.

Horrified, Julie watched as the canoe heaved, bobbled, and tipped, throwing Cindy into the churning water. The girl flailed helplessly, her dark head floating barely above the surface as the gushing, crashing water pushed her ever farther downstream like a helpless leaf or a broken stick until she disappeared beneath the surface completely.

For a few horror frozen seconds nobody moved, then sound exploded into cries and wails and shrieks and everybody galvanized into hurtling action.

"Rob! Jud!" Paul shouted. "Get your life jackets on! Hurry! Come with me!" Paul was already half in a canoe when the two boys joined him. They stroked the water furiously as the current of the rapids caught them and hurled them forward. The metallic taste of fear floated in Julie's mouth as she watched them shoot through the swirling waters.

A wail in her ear made her turn to the trembling, quaking form of Tina. Julie hugged her tightly, trying to soothe her with hollow words she did not believe. It seemed like an eternity passed before Paul and the boys paddled back to the shore where the remainder of the group waited. They had the wayward canoe in tow, but not Cindy.

Drenched, grim, Paul came forward and gathered Julie and the shaking Tina in his arms. Fear had transformed itself into a heavy fist that lay at the pit of Julie's stomach. "Oh, Paul," she whispered, barely able to form the words. "What are we going to do?"

"Steve, get my backpack," Paul ordered. Steve obeyed and Paul took out the walkie-talkie and pressed the "call" button. He transmitted the information and their location crisply, his eyes hard, his voice controlled. The ranger issued a few instructions in static noises over the set.

Paul led the tiny, huddled group over to some rocks and they settled down to await the arrival of the ranger's search team while they prayed. The water droned behind them like a knell.

By the time the rangers arrived in their four-wheel drive vehicles, Paul had covered the area where Cindy had disappeared two more times. There was no sign of her. The rangers quickly fanned out and covered the rapids, too. "There's always the possibility that she made it ashore far downstream," a ranger named Jim told them.

"What should we do now?" Paul asked him.

"I'd take these kids to the nearest town, notify the girl's family, and let us keep looking along the banks."

A sickening shudder swept over Julie. Tess! She didn't even know yet! "Oh, Paul," Julie's voice cracked. Paul reached for her and pulled her close.

"Don't fall apart on me now, honey." His voice was soft, soothing. "I need you Julie. I need you to be with the kids, to keep the lid on things. Tina looks awful."

A look at the girl confirmed Paul's words. Tina's face was a pasty white color. Julie took several deep gulps of air and nodded, pulling back from Paul, staring into his dark blue eyes, understanding his need. They were a team. They had to stick together.

"I guess I'd better ride in with one of the rangers and . . . and make some phone calls," she started.

"We'll move our base of activity down below the rapids," Jim said kindly. "If she got out of the water, she may be somewhere along the banks." He glanced up at the sky. "Only a few more hours of daylight anyway. Once it's dark, we'll have to stop looking until tomorrow."

"The kids . . ." Paul explained. "We're in this thing

together. They want to stay. To help. That boy," he pointed to an ashen-faced Rob, "is the girl's brother."

The ranger shrugged. "It might be a long night. We don't want them getting in the way."

"They won't. They'll set up a small camp. Maybe they can get a fire going. Start some coffee," Paul suggested.

The ranger looked at Paul levelly. "We don't know what we'll find, Mr. Shannon. Or what her condition will be when we do." His implication was ominous.

Julie reached for Paul subconsciously, steeling herself from the dark message of his words. "I—I'd better be going," she stammered.

She climbed into a jeep next to a ranger named Mitch, promising, "I'll call David first. And I'll be back as soon as I can."

Paul nodded and Julie left, dreading the task in front of her, knowing she was going to make the most difficult phone call of her life.

By the time Julie returned with Mitch, the camp had been established down river, a quarter mile from the rapids. A campfire crackled and the tents, retrieved from their trailer, had been erected. Rangers and a few state troopers had setup a command base and were scanning detailed maps of the area.

"How did it go?" Paul asked, taking Julie's hand.

She shuddered, remembering the anguish she'd heard from David and Tess. "David's bringing Tess up immediately," Julie told him.

He glanced at his watch. "It'll be midnight before they arrive. They may not get back here through the woods until dawn."

Rob came over to them. "How's my mom?"

Julie touched the boy's hunched shoulder.

"She's on her way."

"Why?" Rob asked, his eyes angry and pleading. "Why would God let this happen?"

Kindly, Paul said, "Rob, if God's eye is on the spar-

162

row, then all I can tell you is that God has Cindy in His hand, too. You can't lose faith."

At nine o'clock, darkness had fallen so completely that the search was called off until the morning. Julie paced the campsite restlessly. No one really slept, although the kids, the rangers, and the police took turns at trying. By the time the first pale streaks of dawn crossed the sky, the search teams chafed to get started.

After a breakfast cooked over the fire by the girls, Julie supervised the clean-up, anxious to keep busy as the teams separated to search the area along the banks of the river. The sun had scarcely cleared the trees when a jeep pulled into camp with Tess and David.

Julie flew to Tess's side, hugging her tightly, feeling the tension and the fear in her friend's body. Rob grabbed his mother and Paul and David tried to surround them all with comfort and protection from the horror of their reality.

"Tess," Julie started. "Oh, Tess! I'm so sorry." Her voice cracked and Paul took her arm, lending her his strength.

"I—I called Hank," Tess said, her eyes red and swollen, her voice controlled. "He's flying in from California. Don Freytag will drive him over from Washington." She stopped, tightening her trembling voice. "What a way to have a family reunion," she whispered.

The two women held one another for several long moments. "The worst part is not knowing if . . . if she's even alive. . . ." Tess choked.

"She's a child of God," David told them with calm assurance. "He has Cindy with Him. Wherever that is."

Later, privately, Julie walked a short distance from the campsite with David. "What a mess," she told him quietly.

David's thoughtful frown made Julie blurt, "Why didn't someone else from the congregation volunteer for this job last fall?"

"What?"

163

"You know. Maybe if some other couple had been responsible for the kids, this might never have happened. Maybe they could have handled Cindy some other way."

David stopped his walk and turned to look down at her. "What makes you think you and Paul were the only couple to ask to fill in for the Freytags?"

Surprised, Julie stammered, "Y—you chose me and Paul when we were at total odds with each other. I—I just assumed that you had no other choice."

A small smile played at the corners of David's mouth. "I had ten couples volunteer, Julie."

Shock, then embarrassment swept over her. "Why did you pick us?"

"Because God told me to," he said gently. "Because Paul is spiritually mature and you're sensitive. Both of you make up an extraordinarily gifted team to work with these kids." David's words shook her. How alike David and Paul were! Why hadn't she seen that before? How could she have been so blind to Paul's spiritual virtues?

A clamor from the campsite interrupted their conversation as two of the rangers returned. Julie followed David hurriedly. A crowd clustered around them as one held up his prize, a mudcaked, pink tennis shoe. "It's Cindy's!" Tess shouted, running up to the man.

"We found it almost three hundred yards into the woods away from the river."

Julie's heart leaped. "That means she got out!" Paul interjected, as if reading her mind.

"We're sure of it," the ranger confirmed.

"Then she's alive!" Tess cried, clasping her hand over her mouth to stop sobs of relief. "Oh, thank God! She's alive!"

It means we need to find her as soon as possible," Mitch emphasized. "She may be hurt, unable to help us locate her. I'll radio for more troopers. We need to establish more teams, lay out a consistent procedure so that we aren't covering the same ground over and over. Too bad the woods are so dense, or we could call in a helicopter."

In less than an hour, more men arrived. Walkie-talkies and flare guns were issued, maps were passed out, and groups were organized in pairs to systematically fan out in every direction from the point of the discovery of the shoe. Paul took Julie aside. "Want to help?" he asked.

"Could we?"

"I've discussed it with Mitch. He knows I'm a seasoned camper. He said we could be one of the teams."

Julie's heart pounded. She wanted to help. She wanted to do *anything* to find Cindy. The rangers couldn't send out novices, but with Paul she could be a useful member of the search party. "Tell me what I need to do to get ready."

In fifteen minutes, Paul had repacked his backpack with a first aid kit, a blanket, extra clothes, a flashlight, matches, a knife, snack food, and a canteen. Julie quickly donned jeans, T-shirt, flannel shirt, hiking boots and strapped on a second canteen. Mitch issued them a walkie-talkie and gave final instructions.

"Look everywhere. Under bushes, in gulleys, next to rocks. You'd be surprised where a person can crawl off to. If you find her, send us your location according to your compass. You'll probably need help getting her out."

They nodded in unison. "And listen," Mitch warned. "If you find nothing by late afternoon, start back. I mean it," he stressed. "Once daylight goes, you'll be as lost as she is."

Julie swallowed the taste of her own anxiety. *Paul will lead me. He'll do what's safe for both of us.* They went to Tess, Rob, and David before they left and Julie hugged her friend once again. A certain peaceful calm had settled over Tess, and Julie was grateful that David had come with her.

"We'll find her, Tess," Paul's voice said, soft, yet assured.

Tess looked deeply into his eyes through her round-framed glasses. She took his hand and said, "Thank you, Paul." Her voice had a calmness Julie recognized as complete and total trust. Tess continued, her eyes never wavering from his face, "You gave me back one of my children, Paul." Tess glanced over at Rob who sat hunched over an open Bible, then back at Paul, "May God let you bring back my other one."

Quickly, Paul and Julie gathered up their gear and started off into the woods.

CHAPTER 12

THE WOODS STRETCHED UPWARDS in front of Julie and Paul, climbing, ascending, reaching skyward, away from the river as if striving to touch their Creator. The search was slow, tedious, the journey methodical, in a weaving zig-zag that allowed them to cover the mossy, fern-tangled terrain thoroughly. Clusters of wildflowers and clumps of Queen Anne's lace spread out in colorful, lacy fans, while maples and oaks rustled leaf-laden branches in soft green whispers.

Once they covered a sector, Paul marked certain trees with a long gash from his knife. Julie kept her eyes cast ever downward, peering into ferns, behind rock formations, in the hollows of long dead trees, yet, the higher they climbed, the less confident she felt of finding Cindy.

"How could she have wandered so far from the river?" Julie asked Paul as he paused to mark another tree before turning eastward.

"Assuming she's hurt, dazed, who knows?" Paul shrugged his shoulders. "We have to keep going up. She's a strong girl, made more fit by a week of hiking on the mountain trails. She could be anywhere."

Julie fanned out to the west, keeping Paul in her peripheral vision, scanning the forest floor for a clue—a broken branch, a crunched fern, a scrap of cloth—anything that might have heralded Cindy's passage. The hours passed. Shadows lengthened from east to west, until they lay in puddles of late afternoon.

"You hungry?" Paul asked, breaking the hot, languid spell of monotony.

Julie glanced at her watch and was surprised to see it was already four o'clock. The day was almost over and they were no closer to locating Cindy than they'd been that morning. The other search teams had not found her either or they would have been notified via the walkie-talkie. With a weary nod, Julie settled herself against a rock and waited while Paul probed in his backpack for food.

They munched granola bars and dried fruit and sipped water sparingly from the canteen. Julie had long since removed her flannel shirt, knotting the sleeves securely around her waist. A film of perspiration formed on her face and between her shoulder blades, causing her back to itch.

"I can't stand the thought of Cindy having to spend another night alone in the woods." Julie broke the silence with her innermost thought.

"I know. I thought for sure she'd have been found by now."

"How much longer do you think we can search?"

Paul calculated broodingly, "Maybe another hour or two. We have to allow ourselves enough time to get back down to the river and from there to the campsite."

"It stays light until at least nine o'clock," Julie offered hopefully.

A tired smile turned up Paul's mouth. "She's like your own, isn't she, Julie?"

"Yes," Julie confessed, wearily rubbing her neck. "Tess and her kids have been family to me ever since I moved to Washington. I've watched Cindy grow up

168

almost. Ever since she was eleven years old. . . ." Julie stopped, afraid her voice would dissolve into tears.

Paul moved next to her, touching her face and rubbing her cheek tenderly with his thumb. She pressed her cheek into his open palm, fatigue suddenly draining her. The sharp scent of tree resins lingered on his hand and muddled her senses.

She sniffed, pulled back, and searched for a new topic of conversation. "Do you ever hear from Ted and Kathy?"

Paul leaned back against his elbows. "We exchange Christmas cards. They're fine. Live in upstate New York. Ted has a small practice. They have a two year old and another baby on the way."

Julie nodded, imagining their former college friends living in suburbia. Of Kathy, plump and pregnant, chasing after a toddler. A smile traced her lips.

"Do you know what I lived to regret?" Paul asked, watching her, his voice hushed and tender.

She turned questioning eyes into his, momentarily losing herself in the beckoning sapphire coolness. "I wish we would have had that baby." His tone was husky, pensive. "We would have created a beautiful baby, Julie."

Her own voice stuck in her throat and she had to draw away from him because she could not face the eerie sadness his words evoked or the wellspring of heartache from remembering what might have been. She felt a somber sense of loss.

Paul withdrew his hand from her face, cleared his throat and stood rapidly, his attitude brisk. "We'd better keep going." Julie let him pull her to her feet, carefully avoiding his eyes. They resumed their search until the shadows of the woods darkened and deepened and the overhead sky turned from blue to red to plum.

The woods grew quiet and cool. Julie untied her shirt and slipped it on again. Soon, they would have to start back to the campsite. They had failed. They had failed to find Cindy; they had failed to keep their covenant. Somehow, the two episodes became related and intertwined in Julie's mind. Despite all their hopes and plans, they had let down Cindy, each other, and God. For Julie, failure was a bitter brew.

Julie tried to recall the peace and sense of revealed truth she'd felt that morning in the woods. *Was it only a week ago?* Where was her promise to let God lead her? Where was her commitment to follow God's purposes? Where was her understanding of Christian love? A nagging persistent droning sound penetrated her thoughts, nipping and nudging like a bothersome gadfly.

What is it? Water? But they were still miles from the river. Julie paused and listened intently. Yes. She heard the sound of rushing water. Where was it coming from? She turned abruptly, veering north, quickening her pace, searching for the origin of the noise. The ground became rocky, the trees more dense. The scent of fresh water cut through the smell of earth and plant life. She hurried forward, urgently seeking, not knowing why, the source of the scent.

Living water! she thought suddenly, allowing the analogy to quirk the corners of her mouth. The ground was transformed into a sea of ferns, flooding dense and thick, rising in feathery green fingers to touch her jean-clad knees. Julie crashed through them, unaware that she was far from Paul, or that the twilight had descended in deepening shades of purple. She quickened her pace, intent on reaching the water, positive that it held something meaningful for her.

She never saw the edge of the precipice. One moment she was in an ocean of green ferns, the next she was tumbling head over heels down a steep ledge. Her scream pierced the air as she felt herself falling, tumbling, over and down. Julie grasped at the cushion of fern that slid past her, uprooting clumps by the handfuls. She slipped and slid and grasped, breaking the momentum of her fall with the fronds of soft, curling plants.

She half-slid, half-scooted to the floor of a narrow

gully, where she finally landed at the edge of a gurgling, bubbling stream of water. The pebbles felt hard and cold and she struggled backward, feeling the moisture soak through her shirt and into her skin. Shaken, Julie took a quick inventory and found bruises and scrapes but no serious injuries.

She heard Paul calling for her, frantically, high above. "I'm all right!" she shouted. "Be careful! You can't even see the ledge. It just drops off!"

She looked up, squinting. She appeared to be at the bottom of a steep ravine. Ferns and vines covered either side of the tapered gorge, where the stream ran unimpeded through the narrow bottom. She could see a slice of indigo sky overhead, and at the lip of the almost invisible ledge she saw Paul looking down at her.

"Don't move! I'll be right there!"

Julie watched as he scrambled and scooted down the steep incline to reach her. Then he was next to her touching her, stroking her, his eyes wild with anxiety. "Are you all right? Are you sure?"

"Soaking wet," she said, her voice shaking, but light to dispel the fear she saw in his face. "Honest. I'm fine."

"I can get you dry," he said, removing his backpack and probing its interior. He pulled out his flannel shirt and gave it to her. "How'd you find this place anyway?"

She took the shirt, gratefully, trembling in the coolness of the air as twilight and the temperature fell simultaneously. "I heard water running."

"What were you going to do? Turn it off?" His tone was gentle, chiding, allowing her to understand her folly in taking off without telling him.

She fumbled with the buttons on her dripping shirt. Automatically, he reached out to help, his fingers more deft than hers. Color crept up her cheeks as she watched, fascinated. She remembered times from the past when his hands had undressed her with deliberation. Her color deepened and she felt suddenly shy, painfully timid under the intimate gesture of his fingers and the escalating response of her body to them.

"I—I'll do it." She twisted away from him.

His eyes held hers and he stopped himself, awkwardly. "Sure. Sorry." He stood and turned purposely scanning the banks of the ravine while she removed her dripping shirt and donned Paul's dry one.

Painfully, slowly, she rose and straightened to stand by his side. All she saw in either direction was steep, unyielding ground and ever darkening skies. "See a quick escape route?"

He fastened his gaze on her, his eyes flicking over her elfin body in his oversized shirt. She squirmed under his scrutiny. "Too big, huh? Do I look silly?"

Paul jammed his hands into his pockets with something undefinable in his eyes. "It won't be easy to get back up," he told her, ignoring her question. "Are you sure you're okay? Think you can climb?"

Her legs felt rubbery and weak. "Maybe it's less steep further downstream," she suggested, not sure if she could make it to the top.

"Maybe. Let's find out."

They followed the stream southward, in the general direction of the river, hoping it would lead them out. The ravine widened as they traveled, allowing the stream space to flow and spread, but the banks remained steep and unscalable.

"Paul!" Julie stopped suddenly, as an inspiration occurred. "I think I know why we couldn't find Cindy!"

"Why?"

"Don't you see? She did the same thing I did! I'll bet you anything she heard the water and thought it was the river and fell down into this ravine."

A glimmer of understanding flicked across Paul's face. "Maybe you're right."

They began, in earnest, to search the banks of the stream and the thick layers of ferns along its edge. Julie was the first to hear the moan. She crouched and groped through the greenery until her hand hit something firm and warm. It moved! It was alive! "Paul!" she called wildly. "I found her! I found Cindy!"

Quickly, Paul knelt next to her and together they rummaged through the ferns until they uncovered Cindy's limp and whimpering form. Tears spilled down Julie's face as she smoothed Cindy's hair. "Are you all right? Oh, baby . . . are you all right?"

"Julie?" The girl's voice was a cracked whisper. "Is that you, Julie?"

"Yes, honey. It's me and Paul—Mr. Shannon. We've been searching for you all day." She continued to pat and console while Paul ran his long fingers expertly over Cindy's legs and arms.

"Tell me what hurts, Cindy."

The girl winced as he touched her knee and side. The knee was swollen and Paul muttered for Julie to hear, "I think she might have some broken ribs."

Renewed fear clutched at Julie. "What are we going to do?"

"I'm going to hope this walkie-talkie has the range to reach the base camp. You cover her with the blanket in my backpack."

Quickly, Julie obeyed, tucking the blanket snugly around the teen. Cindy was scraped, muddy, her hair a tangle of matted knots. She moaned and took Julie's hand, squeezing it, fearing to release it.

"This is Blue Three," Paul reported into the black communication box using their code name. "We found her! She hurts, but not seriously."

A few seconds of static scratched the air. "We receive you Blue Three," Mitch's voice crackled over the instrument.

Julie expelled her breath in one long sigh. Mitch continued, "Can she walk out?"

"Negative."

A minute of silence followed. Finally, Mitch's voice came through. "We can't come in with a gurney until dawn. Can you manage?"

"Affirmative. I'll build a fire. We'll be all right."

"Can the girl say a few words to her mother?"

Paul held the walkie-talkie next to Cindy's mouth. "Mama? Oh, M—Mama!" She dissolved into sobs. Julie comforted her as Tess's voice sounded from the speaker.

"You rest now, baby. You're safe. I love you, Cindy."

Paul switched off the walkie-talkie. Julie started to move aside, but Cindy's hand shot out to grab her. "Don't go away!"

"I'm not, Cindy. I just want to sponge you off and make you more comfortable."

"Oh, Julie," the girl's eyes welled with renewed tears. "I was so scared! After I got out of the river, I just stumbled around. I didn't know where I was. I didn't know how to get back to the camp."

Julie listened to the teary confession. "I—I got lost. And then I heard the water running and I thought it was the river and I fell," her words poured and tumbled over each other. "I just lay here and prayed that God would help me."

"He did, honey," Julie soothed. "Although I didn't realize it when I fell over the ledge, too. But all the time He was leading us to you."

"I was so cold last night." An involuntary shiver coursed over Cindy.

Julie patted her reassuringly. "It's over now. We're here and you're safe."

Within an hour, darkness enveloped them. Paul built a fire, while Julie tore her flannel shirt into strips and washed Cindy's wounds with water, applying antiseptic and bandages to the more serious ones. She fed the girl small bites of granola bars and offered tiny sips of water. The spreading warmth of the fire comforted them as the darkness of the night clung to the fringes of Paul's makeshift camp.

"I—I really made a mess of things, didn't I?" Cindy's voice was contrite, miserable as Julie tucked the blanket under her for the night.

"Yes, you did," Julie confirmed, stroking Cindy's forehead with affection. "Why did you run away?"

Again, tears pooled in the teen's eyes shimmering in the reflected light of the fire. "I—I just felt so *betrayed!* I mean, Jud and Tina . . . she was my best friend." Cindy choked out the words, painfully.

Julie's own eyes welled with empathic tears. *I know! I know!* Betrayed. How well she knew what betrayal felt like. How well she remembered the sense of loss, the feelings of hurt and vengeance and loneliness. From some deep pit inside herself, Julie responded to Cindy's anguish. Surprisingly, her voice sounded calm and soft, even to her own ears. "But running away never solved anything, Cindy," she said. "I know from experience that it only makes things worse. Sometimes," she dabbed at Cindy's tears, "facing the problem is the first step toward healing."

The light of revelation spread through her. Running away. Hadn't that been how she had solved her problem? Wasn't that exactly how she had responded to her sense of betrayal and loss?

Cindy sighed and nodded. She held Julie's hand and slowly drifted off to sleep, relaxing her grip as she floated deeper and deeper into sleep's safe haven. Julie extricated her hand and walked closer to the fire, sitting cross-legged and staring into its orange yellow depths.

From far away, she heard an owl call. Insects buzzed, hummed, chirped, and croaked in a night symphony of music. She glanced across the flickering flames and saw Paul watching her, his face haloed in the firelight, all planes and sharp angles, his eyes mirroring the yellow of the flames.

Their gazes met and locked, holding them prisoners by a tether of oneness, a cord of unity. He broke the silence first. "I heard what you told Cindy—about running away. Were you talking about us?"

"Yes. Running away made no sense for Cindy two

days ago. Or for me . . . five years ago. I'm so sorry I did that. I'm sorry I never gave us another chance."

Paul closed his eyes briefly. A small smile played over his mouth. "I have a confession to make," he told her quietly. "Last September, when I came to Washington, I told you it was just for a job. That wasn't exactly true."

He stood and Julie watched him cross to stand in front of her. "I wanted to make peace with you, Julie. More than anything, I wanted you to forgive me."

A lump rose in her throat and she had to avert her eyes so he wouldn't see the sadness and the longing in them that she felt. "I forgive you, Paul."

He dropped next to her and circled her shoulders with his arm, pulling her close to his side. "I've wanted to tell you something for a very long time." He chose his words carefully, picking his way through the ruins of their past memories carefully, avoiding the rubble of old hurts, old wounds. "What happened with Bianca . . . it had nothing to do with love. And frankly, it didn't have anything to do with sex either." He paused and the fire snapped and crackled punctuating the air.

"It had everything to do with power and ambition. I wanted it. She had it. She offered and I took. In the end, I lost everything."

With his words, Julie saw his face as if a veil had dropped from her eyes. She saw his pain, his soul-rending anguish. She trembled at the undisguised intensity of his hurt. Until that moment, she had never thought of Paul as being wounded by his actions. Now she knew that he had been.

"In a matter of days, I lost everything that I had ever loved. My wife, career, home . . . all of it. Everything I had struggled to build all my life. But it wasn't Bianca Rinaldi that took it from me, Julie. It was *me* that did it."

At the mention of Bianca's name, Julie waited for the familiar pangs to shoot through her. For the familiar pictures to accost and torment her brain. But, oddly, they did not. The raw gaping wound on her heart no longer throbbed and hurt. The agony had evaporated. In its place was the revelation of her own lack of mercy and empathy for Paul. She'd locked her heart off from him, intent on punishing him, never perceiving his hurts or his needs.

"Forgive . . . me . . . Paul. . . ." Her voice broke.

The set line of his mouth softened. Tenderness leaped from his eyes. "It was necessary, Julie. Don't you see? As long as I looked to myself for my strength, Christ couldn't get into my life. But when I was at the bottom of the pit, I saw Him. And that changed my life forever."

Paul had seen light. She had seen darkness. He had turned toward God. She had turned away. The revelation stunned her. She felt loss. *Why is that?* Julie asked herself. *Why do I feel loss when the Bible tells me to count all things as gain?*

The new idea made her catch her breath. For a moment, she'd looked upon their past as failure instead of God's sovereignty over their lives. In reality, she had gained a great deal through her marriage to Paul. She'd gained love! A deep, passionate, and profound human love that few women ever experience in a lifetime. And Paul had loved her in the same way. What she'd lost was her vision of walking in God's will.

Very purposefully, she lay her head against the hollow of his shoulder and listened to the thumping of his heart. His cheek rested against the top of her head, his arm tightened, securing her in his grip.

"I came to Washington to make peace with you, Julie. God has been faithful to give us that. I can leave now knowing that you're fine. That God has you safely in His care. That the past is truly dead." His voice sounded husky and distant, as if coming from the end of a long tunnel.

She watched as fireflies flickered in the air above them. Little pinpricks of light, chemically coded messages of love. "Find me. Find me." "Here I am. Here I am."

Warmed by the fire, tucked in the circle of Paul's arms, Julie felt her eyes grow heavy and her limbs languid. She wanted to move but couldn't. She felt too tired, too lazy. Her last conscious thought as sleep reached out and took her was that she loved Paul Shannon. Still.

CHAPTER 13

SOMETHING NAGGING AND PERSISTENT kept tugging
Julie out of the warm folds of sleep. She twisted, and
swatted at it with her hand, but, in the end, her eyes
popped open in confused, disgruntled awareness. She
was curled in a ball, her head buried in Paul's lap and
it was Paul who was nudging her out of her comfort.

"It's time to rise and shine, sleepyhead."

She sat up and blinked, seeing the dying embers of
the fire and the gray of the sky. The foliage drooped
moist and heavy with dew. The stream gurgled, splash-
ing icily over smooth stones. Cindy slept soundly, the
blanket clutched under her chin like a small child.

Julie stretched, realizing that her comfort had been
an illusion. In actuality, her muscles were cramped and
sore. "Did I sleep on your lap all night?" she asked,
self-conscious and contrite at forcing him to spend an
uncomfortable night, nestling her instead of stretching
out and resting.

His blue eyes twinkled and his overnight growth of
beard made him look decidedly sexy to her. She warred
against the impulse to reach up and flip his curls off

his forehead. "As usual, it was a pleasure to sleep with you," he mused.

She stood and shook out her stiff limbs. "You certainly know how to show a girl a good time," she bantered and stooped by the stream where she splashed her face vigorously with the biting cold water.

Paul's rich, deep laugh broke the air and Cindy stirred at the noise. Julie tended her lovingly, assuring her that a rescue team would arrive shortly with the gurney. A few minutes later, the crackle of the walkie-talkie confirmed Julie's words. Paul gave Mitch compass coordinates and throughout the next hour offered sporadic directions via the instrument to the approaching party.

The three of them waited, nibbling on the remainder of the dried fruit. Julie's stomach growled in protest. "I'm going to eat a bear when I get out of here," she told them. "After a hot shower."

They watched the sky turn pink then red as the sun painted its way leisurely into the heavens. Trees soared over the sides of the gully, straight and green, filling the breeze with damp smells of leaves and summer flowers. A butterfly fluttered around their campsite, its translucent wings vibrating joyously in the gleaming morning light.

Finally, the rescue team with its gurney arrived. "How'd you get down there?" Mitch yelled from above them, his massive body leaning perilously close to the edge of the overhang.

"I tripped!" Julie yelled. "But look what we found at the bottom!"

A broad smile split Mitch's rugged face. "Hang on. It may take a while to get down there with this thing."

Four rangers lumbered downward, carefully picking through the damp ferns. Once arrived, Mitch tossed Paul a thermos of hot coffee and directed his men in strapping Cindy onto the canvas sling that would carry her out.

"There's a lot of relieved people back at the camp, little lady," Mitch told Cindy. "A great bunch of kids waiting to see you, too. They've been praying constantly for you for two days and nights."

She offered him a wan smile.

"Coffee never smelled so good!" Julie said, taking the steaming red-handled lid from Paul's hands. She took a long swallow, letting the scalding black fluid rejuvenate her tired mind. She gave the cup to Paul, and watched him drink, the steam curling around his face. An old, long dormant memory floated up to invade her consciousness. She thought about another morning, another hot cup of coffee.

"Breakfast in bed. How cavalier!"

Paul bowed from the waist and presented the tray to her. Two mugs of coffee and a rosebud in a silver vase greeted her eyes. "Yes, milady."

Julie giggled and clapped her hands gleefully. "Two cups? I couldn't possibly drink two cups at once."

"I could be persuaded to join you." His sapphire colored eyes danced in the bright morning sunshine as it flooded across the rumpled sheets of their bed.

"Is this standard operating procedure for our honeymoon? Or will it pass as you grow tired and bored with me?" Her voice took on a teasing, come-hither quality.

Paul's robe, tied loosely at his waist, parted to expose his muscled chest as he bent and took the coffee cup out of her hands.

"Hey! Indian giver! That's mine."

He lowered himself next to her on the bed and traced his finger along the side of her face, down her neck to where a vein pulsed in her throat. She caught her breath and trembled expectantly.

"And you are mine," he said, claiming her mouth with his. "Always and forever. You are mine."

The gurney had ascended, leaving Paul and Julie to erase the signs of their campfire, pack their gear and follow. By now, the sun had reached into the crevices of the ravine and rapidly warmed the air. Julie watched as Paul crouched to repack his backpack. Mesmerized, she followed the movement of his hands as they folded and stuffed items into the nylon pouch.

As soon as they reached civilization they would be inundated with people. Mitch had informed them that a group of reporters was waiting to interview them when they arrived at the camp. Soon everything would change. Everything.

She would go home. She would resume work. Paul would leave Washington. He'd go away to rebuild his life in another city. Just as she would rebuild hers. They'd start over, fresh, unencumbered by their past. They were free. Separate. Divided. Apart.

"All set?" he asked from his crouched position.

"Don't go."

"Are you kidding?" His laugh was congenial. "If we don't get up that embankment, they'll be sending a rescue party after us and. . . ." His voice trailed away and he straightened slowly, fixing her with his gaze as the deeper meaning of her words penetrated his mind. "What did you say, Julie?"

Her heart thudded wildly against her ribs. Her stomach quivered and her mouth tasted arid and parched. "Don't go, Paul. Please don't leave me."

He crossed to her with three long-legged strides, scooped her up in his arms and crushed her against his chest. The force of his embrace drove the stale air out of her lungs and she closed her eyes, while a flood of emotions built and bubbled within her.

"I love you, Paul." Her words tumbled out like water over a dam. "I've always loved you. I always will." Her voice cracked and tears trickled down her cheeks. "You're my husband."

He buried his face in her hair and his arms refused to release her. "Julie. . . ." His voice sounded strangled. "I love you, baby. How I love you!"

Laughing, crying, shaking, she kissed him hungrily, reveling in the taste of his mouth, the strength of his arms, the scratch of his beard on her face. She felt a

182

unique oneness with him, a deep sense of physical and spiritual belonging.

"We'll build things right this time, Julie," Paul promised, drawing her to arms' length, looking down at her in the gathering pools of yellow sunlight. "David will help. And we'll build things on the foundation of rock. No more sand," he said, squeezing her shoulders.

He gazed at her lovingly for a long minute before he finally asked, "Are you ready to climb?"

Julie took a deep breath. "I'm ready."

He took her hand and pulled her toward the steep, jutting embankment. She followed behind him, scrambling and struggling to ascend the slippery slope. Her feet slid, but she clung to the foliage and stepped in the path that Paul cleared for her. The climb was slow and difficult, and when they finally emerged into the sea of whispering ferns at the top of the precipice, Julie collapsed in a gasping heap, her legs weak and rubbery.

"Here," Paul said, dropping his backpack to the ground and wrapping his arms around her for support. "Rest against me."

She did, breathing in deep, shuddering gulps of air to cool her burning lungs. She leaned against him, waiting for her strength to return. She locked her arms around his waist and laid her head against his hard chest. She felt his heart hammering. She heard its steady rhythm. And something in her spirit said, *Home*.

Home. Julie had come home. The unraveled string of her life had come together again, forming, from the long and twisting thread, a full circle. In Paul's arms, the ends touched and fused. "Take me home," she whispered against his chest.

And he did.

About the Author

Lurlene McDaniel has over one million books in print for the Young Adult market. Her series, *One Last Wish,* was recently launched by Bantam Books, following a string of successful titles dealing with teens facing life-threatening and life-altering events. Credited with carving out a new genre in the YA marketplace, Lurlene structures her works with a strong emphasis on Biblical values and ethics.

She is also Fiction Editor for *Faith 'n Stuff: The Magazine for Kids,* a Guideposts publication, and a frequent speaker and teacher at writing workshops and conferences. In the past, she has written numerous advertising, radio, and television commercials, as well as a magazine column.

Two of her novels were CBC/IRA Children's Choice Award winners, one has been awarded a RITA for Best YA of 1991 for Romance Writers of America, and one has been placed in a literary time capsule at the Library of Congress to be opened in 2089.

Lurlene has two grown sons and makes her home in Chattanooga, TN.

Forever Romances are inspirational romances designed to bring you a joyful, heart-lifting reading experience. If you would like more information about joining our Forever Romance book series, please write to us:

Guideposts Customer Service
39 Seminary Hill Road
Carmel, NY 10512

Forever Romances are chosen by the same staff that prepares *Guideposts,* a monthly magazine filled with true stories of people's adventures in faith. *Guideposts* is not sold on the newsstand. It's available by subscription only. And subscribing is easy. Write to the address above and you can begin reading *Guideposts* soon. When you subscribe, each month you can count on receiving exciting new evidence of God's Presence, His Guidance and His limitless love for all of us.